Papatong

An anthology of short stories
set in Indonesia and beyond

by
David Powell Davies

This is an anthology of short stories.
First published in October 2018
by Tambourine Press Ltd
5 Harringay Gdns, London, N8 0SE

ISBN 978-0-9576122-9-7

Front cover designed by Freya Newmarch, artist.

Papatong

An anthology of short stories
set in Indonesia and beyond

by

Tambourine
Press

David Powell Davies

The idea for this book was discussed with David in March 2018. He had been writing these stories for many years, since moving to Indonesia in 2003.

He was born with a gift of laughter and a sense that the world was mad."
— Rafael Sabatini, Scaramouche

Dave's greatest talents – his story-telling and ability to make everyone laugh.

A Davies

Tambourine Press

Octoberr 2018

Table of Contents

CLICKETTY CLACK

Click, clack, clicketty clack like a railway engine racing down the track, mum's fingers flew over the piece of cloth guiding the needle as it plunged in and out while her foot pumped the pedal up and down. Hunched over the old Singer sewing machine her concentration was so intense her eyes seemed to be almost scorching the material.

She came to the end of a run, glanced up and saw me quietly standing there, watching her. A smile lit her face and all the lines and furrows disappeared. Mum stood up and stretched. For a brief moment she looked like our cat 'Jewel', the same sort of way of pushing out with her arms.

'Hungry?' she asked.

I grinned. When was I ever not hungry!

She came over and gave me a hug and I could smell that lovely warm smell of her. It was a fragrant, inviting smell of spices from cooking, wood smoke, and soap.

We went into the kitchen and mum started to chop vegetables to fry with some rice. I watched her closely, my tummy rumbling. She splashed soy sauce into the wok and the smell of the food cooking was delicious.

'Pass me the mushrooms?' she asked. I went to the vegetable rack and looked for them. Outside people started shouting and then I heard the village bell ringing.

Mum froze and turned her head, listening.

'Wait here, don't move!' she said to me, the urgency in her voice frightening me, then she ran outside.

I could hear lots of voices now, many people were calling out and there were shouts of warning. I began to feel worried as something about all the sounds was wrong. They weren't the normal village sounds. Even when people quarreled or had arguments they were normal sounds. Our next-door neighbours, Pak and Ibu Sih, were always fighting. Me and my friends would stand outside and listen. Once Ibu Sih looked out her window and saw us. She came rushing out and chased us away. Then she went back inside and threw bananas at her husband.

What I was hearing now was different. There was a smell of fear in the voices. I heard my mother ask, 'Where are they?' She sounded strange, I almost didn't recognize her voice.

'About 30 minutes away,' someone replied. The warning bell in the village was still ringing. This was the first time I'd heard it like this. It had rung before of course when someone died or got married but this was different. The sound was sharp and piercing - it made me jump and I started to feel scared.

I started towards the door just as mum burst back into the kitchen.

'Quick get your blanket from your bedroom,' she said as she threw water on the cooking fire.

'What's happening?' I asked. 'Why is everyone shouting and why is the bell ringing?'

'No time now' she said, grabbing bits of food and pushing them into a bag.

'Get your blanket now and mine. I'll explain later.'

I ran to do as I was told as mum grabbed a piece of canvas that we used to sit on if the ground was damp. I got the blankets and was coming out of a bedroom when mum called.

'Sweetheart, quickly help me please.'

I ran to her and saw her lifting her sewing

machine.

'Help me carry this to the well,' she said.

There was something about her voice and whole manner that made me keep my mouth shut and just do as she asked. After we got it to the well, mum tied a long length of rope to it and we both let it gently down into the water. When it reached the bottom, mum tied a piece of string to the end of the rope and let the rope drop into the water. Then leaning over the edge of the well she tied the string to a nail in the wall of the well. You couldn't see it! It was the same colour as the cement.

'Right let's go,' she said and I followed her at a run.

It seemed like everyone had gone crazy. People were running in all directions, some women wailing and screaming, children were crying and all the time the bell calling out its warning. I ran behind mother as she quickly went through the village and started up the mountain into the jungle. Some people were shouting now.

'The soldiers are coming! The soldiers are coming!'

Then I understood. We all knew that there were soldiers from another country in our land. We children had heard the grown-ups talking about the terrible things these soldiers had done in the towns and other villages. How they had smashed, broken and burnt their way through our beautiful island of Java. How they had hurt people, tortured and even killed them. Our village was safe though, wasn't it? I mean there were no towns near us. There was no reason for soldiers to come to our village. We were safe weren't we? Or that's what we had thought and now they were here. The soldiers were coming and we were running into the jungle.

It had rained the day before and the ground was still wet and muddy. I slipped but before I hit the ground, mother's hand shot out and grabbed me yanking me up.

'We must get into the jungle quickly before they come' she said.

I looked at her as I clutched the blankets to my chest and then I started to cry. Not loudly, just the tears running down my face, I couldn't stop them. Mum crouched down and wrapped her arms round me.

'Oh my darling boy,' she said. 'Don't be frightened, everything will be alright. I won't let anything happen to us. I need you to be a brave boy.' She wiped the tears from my face. 'I need you to help me, can you do that?'

I took a deep breath. 'Yes mum'.
She gave me a big grin and I grinned back.

'That's my brave boy.' Then she stood up.

'Now come on, run!'

We both ran into the enveloping jungle.

We stayed in the jungle for a week. Using big leaves to shelter us from the rain and sleeping on the canvas huddled under our blankets. What food mum had brought soon ran out but we dug up roots and ate them. We found a pond with clear water which we could drink. We couldn't risk a fire to cook anything just in case there were any soldiers nearby. After a week we decided to go back to the village not knowing what we would find.

We could smell the burning before we saw any buildings. Mum gripped my hand tightly and her face was set hard. Then we came to Pak Asep's house on the outskirts of the village. Only there wasn't a house anymore just burnt ground. I heard Mum cry out and then I saw why. Pak Asep was lying twisted on the ground in front of what was left of his house. I knew he was dead. He was horribly burnt! The wind gusted up blowing the smell of his body towards us. Mum and I both turned away and were violently sick. Mum tried to shield my eyes, but I saw. I saw and I smelt and I knew the memory of that stench would remain with me for the rest of my life.

I remembered then how kind Pak Asep had been to me and mum after daddy died. He had worked our rice field for us giving mum a chance to get a little sewing business together. He made little toys for me and did things for mum in the house. My favourite toy was a little boat made out of bits of tin. If you put a tiny shred of kapok in it and lit it, the hot air would blow out of the end of the boat making it move on the water. I also remembered how proud Pak Asep had been of his little house. He loved it. He had stayed with his house. He had not run to the jungle and now he was dead.

Then we came to the rest of the village. It was terrible. The soldiers had taken stuff and just thrown it into the street, smashing it up. Some of the houses they had burned. There were people we knew crying and wandering about not knowing what to do. When we got to our house I couldn't believe what the soldiers had done. All our clothes, the mattresses from our beds were lying scattered outside. They had been ripped and the kapok filling was wet, soggy and dirty brown in the mud.

Inside it was worse. Nothing was untouched. Cups, plates, photographs all were broken. They had even slashed and kicked in the bamboo walls of the house. Mum bent down, picked up a broken frame and gently removed the photograph. It was of her and daddy when they got married. A muddy boot had left its mark. She dusted it softly with her hands. Then she broke down. The tears came first and splashed on the photograph causing little brown rivulets to run down it. Then her body started to shake as great wracking sobs tore out of her. All I could do was run to her and hold her as hard as I could. After a while she grew quiet and stopped shaking. I felt her smooth my hair and pat me gently on my back.

'Thank you my darling boy' she said 'thank you.' Holding my hand she led me out of the house. I followed her to the well, where she leaned over and found the string tied to the nail. She gave a big sigh of satisfaction and started to pull the string out of the well. Eventually the rope appeared.

'Help me,' she said and we both pulled on the rope together.

In a short while the sewing machine broke the surface of the water and soon we lugged it up and over the edge of the well. There seemed to be nothing wrong with it.

'Good,' said mum. 'All I have to do is dry and oil it and it will work like new.' She looked at me and smiled at the confused look on my face. 'This was the last present your daddy gave me before he died.'

Much later as I cleaned and swept up some of the mess, I heard 'click, clack, and clicketty clack'. The sewing machine! Mum had got it working again! I ran to the sound and saw that she was making new covers for the mattresses. She looked up and smiled.

'We'll sleep on soft beds tonight,' she said.

There was a knock on our door or on what was left of it. Some of our neighbours were standing outside with blankets and sheets that needed repairing. They had brought food and wood for the fire to pay for the work. I remember thinking then that life carried on, no matter what. The soldiers thought they had defeated us when they broke our village but they could never do that. They could hurt us but never conquer us. They would never defeat my mother!

'Click, clack, clicketty clack'.

I listened to the sound and I felt a deep sadness and anger inside me. The soldiers had not defeated us, but they had taken my childhood.

This story is based on actual events as told to David by his Indonesian mother-in-law.

GUNUNG KAWI

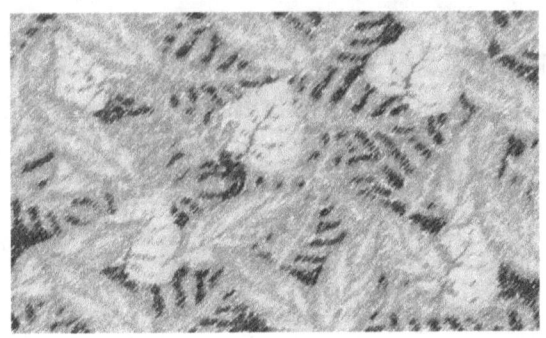

The mountain loomed ahead of me. The morning mists still clung to the top of Gunung Kawi and trickled down the sides. The sky was uniformly grey but it was not the grey of a pending storm which builds and swirls gathering its power rather it was an opaque fog that asphyxiated the sky. A dull blanket obscuring the sun that I knew was there. The warm air clung oppressively to my skin and already I was beginning to regret this whole insane venture.

Once upon a time, this magnificent result of volcanic upheaval had been heavily forested but that was way in the past. Ignorant people had chopped, hacked and removed the trees carving the remaining soil into plots of land to grow rice and vegetables. Then the rains came and without the protection of the trees and their roots, the soil was washed away year by year. So now there were no crops, no trees and no soil, just rock. I stopped for a breather and looked up, God, I was so out of condition. My neck itched and I had the curious impression that someone was watching me. I turned but could see no one, just black rock.

Nobody lived on the mountain; it stood bleak and deserted a monument to stupidity and ignorance. The present mists obscured the entrance to a cave near the summit until the sun grew hot enough to break through and burn them off. To say it was deserted was not quite accurate; someone lived in that cave. This hermit like figure was my destination, .In the Indonesian language he was known as an 'orang pintar', a 'clever man', a 'kuncen' or 'dukun', a person who could grant gifts and was practiced in the dark arts. People believed they were able to converse with and control demons and spirits. If you wanted anything whether it was money, power, control over another person, whatever your desire, the 'orang pintar' could supply it and make it happen, at a price. However be careful what you ask for as the price might be too high.

Many are the tales whispered in the kampungs of Java of the terrible results of the greed and need that led people to climb those rocky slopes. Yet still they came. If you were lucky, you paid with animals, a single sacrifice or a monthly commitment. Or maybe the price would be a child, maybe your child. A 'Buta', a huge genie like spirit would come and take your child. How could anyone give their child? What in God's name could be more valuable than your child? How desperate would you have to be?

It is so easy to judge. Most people live lives of stultifying mundanity. The emotional range of their existence is within a narrow, tightly held band. What a waste, what a glorious, unforgivable waste. I smiled wryly to myself as these thoughts passed through my head. Who is judging now, Jonathan?

Sometimes a supplicant paid with their age and a spirit would take some of their life. If you were young, losing five or ten years at the end of your life, it did not seem such a big deal if the prize was big enough; it was too far away to really worry about. But as you grew older and your life grew shorter, what you had done would return to haunt you.

A husband and wife coming together might agree to share their home with a 'Tuyul', a 'spirit boy'. At first this did not seem too terrible a price to pay but little did they realize that they would be sharing their lives with a demon that would suck on the wife's nipples during the dark nights tearing their lives apart and for what?

Don't judge Jonathan. Who knows what wretched despair led them to wearily climb this mountain as you are doing now?

A voice inside me said, 'turn back, turn back', but my urgency drove me on. I grew ever closer to the cave on the mountain. Slung over my shoulder was a canvas sack which contained the bananas, rice and flowers as an offering to the kuncen. More importantly though it also held the black cockerel whose throat would be cut and whose warm blood the kuncen would drink in the ritual. My hand went protectively to my shirt pocket which contained a recent photograph of my nephew, Simon who was the reason for this whole deranged journey but it had to be done. Steel yourself Jonathan, steel yourself.

The rice fields that lay around the foot of 'Gunung Kawi' belied the evil that infested the rock that towered above them. They looked healthy and lush, eye soothingly green. Ironically this was mostly due to the nutrient rich soil washed down from the sides of the mountain. As soon as I set foot on the rough trail that climbed to the cave of the kuncen, I felt a deep, draining weariness take hold of me. Again a voice in me said, 'turn back, turn back fool' but I had come too far since that fateful day two months previously in Jakarta when a chance meeting had set me on this course.

'Jonathan, how's your drink? Let me refresh it for you. I'd like you to meet Dr. Mamet. He's an expert on Black Magic and all that nonsense that you seem so fascinated by. Dr. Mamet.'

As my friend called the name, a tall, bespectacled and rather fat Indonesian turned to look at us. I was immediately struck by his eyes. They were deep, dark and unfathomable. I shivered slightly. Silly really, but there was something about the man that was distant and cold, unreachable almost.

'Yes, Mr. Roberts, a successful party I think.'

His voice was a quiet, sibilant lisp, quite unexpected and comical. I laughed, unable to stop myself.

'You find something funny?' he asked me.

'Yes, I mean no', I said.

He smiled but it was a smile of hidden humour and not the smile of shared laughter.

'My friend Jonathan is interested in all that mumbo jumbo you're interested in Mamet. Excuse me; I'm needed by my wife.'

Then my friend moved away leaving me with the enigmatic Doctor.

'So do you think it is 'mumbo jumbo' Mr....?'

'Peters,' I replied, 'Jonathan Peters. I don't know what is meant by 'mumbo jumbo'.'

'I think our host was using it in a disparaging fashion. The black arts, voodoo, spirits, ghosts, things that go bump in the night,' lisped Mamet.

I smiled. 'Yes I think he was. He's rather a pragmatic man, prosaic almost.'

'Unimaginative you mean.'

I smiled again, this time at the judgment. For the way Mamet said it, it was a judgment, a damning summing up in one dismissive word.

'There are more things Horatio in Heaven and Earth, than are yet dreamed of.' I replied.

'Hamlet,' said Mamet. 'Yes indeed Mr. Peters a very apt quote but you have forgotten Hell.'

'Hell? Do you mean the hell of fire and brimstone, demons and perpetual scorching punishment?' I countered.

'Is that what you believe in Mr. Peters?

'No it isn't,' I snapped at him, slightly waspishly. His condescending manner was beginning to annoy me. 'I believe hell is whatever we create for ourselves, a kind of mental or psychic flagellation if you like.'

Mamet smiled and nodded. I couldn't tell if he agreed or disagreed; that was the disconcerting thing about him. He was a closed book, he revealed nothing.

'Have you heard about Gunung Kawi?' he asked.

'No, what is it?'

'It's a mountain in Jawa Timur.'

'That's Eastern Java, isn't it?'

'Yes. A holy man lives in a cave at the summit of the mountain. Well perhaps holy is the wrong description, a more accurate one would be, now how would you say it in your language, necromancer?'

I laughed at the quaintness of the word, the old fashioned use of it. His face hardened.

'He is certainly nothing to laugh at,' he said.

'I'm sorry; I wasn't laughing at you or him more at the unexpected use of the word.'

'What would you call someone who communes with devils and spirits?' he asked.

'A fool,' I replied. He barked or rather I should say he laughed but it was short and sharp like a dog.

'Indeed Mr. Peters if you or I were to communicate with the underworld we would be considered fools but the 'orang pintar' on Gunung Kawi well he …' And here he just stopped and smiled, letting his answer trail into damnable nothingness.

Whether intentionally or not, this frustrating man had me hooked, I wanted to know more.

You see Brian Roberts was quite correct about my interest in magic. Not the magic of the trickster magician but the darker and more sinister magic of evil versus good, the magic of Satan versus God. Oh yes I believe in Satanic forces, the power of the dark lord, if you like and also in the power of light. Which is more powerful? Well there's the rub. I have to believe that good is more powerful than evil, we have to, don't we? But sometimes I catch myself wondering whether it is a desperate, snatching at straws sort of belief and that evil is the stronger. This was the problem, my faith was weak and I knew I was susceptible to persuasion.

Was I gullible? No, I had quite a jaundiced view of life however I prided myself on always being open to a variety of points of view and opinions and this was my undoing.

Mamet drew himself to his full height, which I noticed once more was quite considerable, and cast his eyes around the room. His lips were curled in distaste at what he could see. He placed his drink, which he had barely touched, on a small, ceramic, side table. His hands fluttered briefly in a dismissive gesture as though brushing off the residue of something unpleasant around him and then he moved towards the exit.

'Dr Mamet,' I called out and hurried after him. He stopped and turned, looking quizzically at me, waiting. To my annoyance I found myself stammering at the sudden realisation that I did not know what to say.

'I... I... may I speak with you again, there are one or two things I would like to ask you.' I finished quite lamely.

He looked at me appraisingly, curiously, then nodded sharply. 'Yes,' he said. Then turned and left the room.

I stood there hovering like a fool and realised he had given me no phone number to contact. Damn! Now I would have to get his number from Brian and I felt uncomfortable about that.

'Jonathan, has Mamet gone already?' Brian startled me out of my reverie. I put down my empty glass on the tray he was carrying and helped myself to another drink.

'Yes, he has, odd fellow, isn't he? Just put down his glass and left, just like that. Damned annoying as I had one or two things I needed to ask him. You don't happen to have his telephone number do you?' I asked casually as if it was an afterthought and felt myself blush at my subterfuge.

'Ah I thought you two would get along. He's as daft as you are about all that black magic nonsense.'

I felt a flash of irritation and annoyance at Brian's dismissal and ignorance of what to me was a fascinating subject but concealed it behind a throwaway laugh.

'Oh good Lord no nothing like that. In fact I found him decidedly weird, but he did mention one or two people that might be useful business contacts.'

God how easy it is to lie.

'Ah business eh?' Brian tapped the side of his nose in a conspiratorial fashion. 'That's the only reason I stay in touch with him, he does seem to know a staggering number of influential people. Follow me.' He led me to the telephone table in the hallway.

It was a couple of weeks after Brian's party and I still had not contacted Mamet. I had done my homework and checked up on the man and also made enquiries about Gunung Kawi and the 'orang pintar' that lived there. Everything I had heard was negative and full of warning.

I had been to see a skin specialist about an annoying rash that just would not heal and also the growth of some moles on my body. The doctor had looked serious when he looked at them. He'd decided to send me up for a biopsy. I was waiting for the results when I received a phone call from my sister that completely turned my world upside down.

I knew something was wrong as soon as I answered the phone. 'What's up Jennie?' I asked. I heard the choke in her voice that threatened to break her tight control.

'It's Simon, Jonathan.' She paused and I could hear her breathing deeply to control her emotions. 'The doctors have confirmed lymphatic cancer, stage two.'

I stood in bewilderment at this unreal dose of Universal judgment. 'Jonathan are you there?'

'Oh my darling, I'm so sorry. I'm stunned by your damnable, awful news. This is very sudden; he seemed fine when I saw you all a few weeks ago. In fact, he was full of beans.'

'Yes, shortly after that he came home from school and complained about feeling tired. John and I didn't think anything of it; we just thought he'd been overdoing it a bit.' She sighed. 'But he didn't improve and became even more listless and completely without any energy.'

'That's certainly not like the Simon I know, the little scamp.'

'I know,' Jennie managed a chuckle. 'That's why we decided on a checkup. The doctors called us in and gave us the news yesterday.'

She broke then and started sobbing down the phone. I couldn't stand it. I am the weak, vacillating fool and was always the despair of our parents whereas Jennie was always the strong one. She knew what she wanted out of life and invariably got it. I had never heard her like this. It tore my heart out.

'Where's John?' I asked, desperate for some way to stop her wailing pain.

'Gone to work.' She was sniffling and blowing her nose.

'Gone to work?' I couldn't keep the surprise out of my voice.

'I told him to,' she said. 'He's completely in pieces and I thought it might give him something to focus on.'

How typical of Jennie. In the midst of her own agony still taking care of others.

'Right, I'm coming round,' I said. 'Where's Simon now?'

'He's sleeping,' she said. 'Thank you Jonathan.' I made no mention of my own problems. They seemed insignificant now.

Shortly after, the germ of an idea began to grow in my mind. A crazy, impossible idea but the more I thought about it, the more I became convinced that this was what I had to do. For once in my useless life, I had a chance to do something worthwhile.

I phoned Mamet up and made an appointment to see him.

'Mr. Peters,' he said in that strange sibilant lisp as later he led the way into his lounge, 'How interesting that you should call.'

I decided to get straight to the point. 'Mr. Mamet,' I said. 'At that party where we met, you mentioned a mountain called Gunung Kawi.'

He nodded.

I continued quickly before my nerve failed me. 'You also mentioned an 'orang pintar' I think you called him, who lives on that mountain and has certain powers.'

Again he nodded and waited for me to continue. Why did I feel that he was holding out the rope to hang me?

'What I want to know is what this man can do or is it all just hocus pocus?'

'What exactly do you want Mr. Peters?' he asked.

'I want to trade my life for my nephew's health. Can he do that?'

There was a long silence. He indicated a chair. 'Please sit down Mr. Peters and tell me everything.' When I had finished, he looked at me inquisitively, penetratingly. 'You do realize what you are asking,' he eventually said. 'Once you have committed yourself there can be no going back.'

'Yes,' I replied.

'You must tell me exactly what you want and I will record your wishes in Indonesian on a cassette tape which you will play to the orang pintar. I will tell you how to get there and what to take.' He paused and then again looked curiously at me. 'Why are you doing this?'

'I told you,' I replied. 'A small boy's life is at stake.'

'Well Mr. Peters you are either a fool or a very brave man, perhaps both. I will assist you in what you want. But I still cannot understand why you are doing this?'

I shrugged, there was no answer. I knew what he meant. It must have seemed unbelievable that I was willing to give up my life. There was a payback however, one that he could not understand. I was Simon's uncle and godfather and I would do whatever I could to save him. For once my life had purpose and it was that purpose that now drove me to put one foot in front of the other towards the cave on Gunung Kawi.

The clouds parted and then closed again almost immediately but in that short moment I could see the opening to the cave, a dark, forbidding hole in the rock. I hesitated for a second and could feel my fear welling up inside me, threatening to make me turn and run back down the way I had come. I pulled out Simon's photograph and looked at his cheeky, smiling face. My fear ebbed away to be replaced with a new found determination and I set off once more on the final leg of the climb.

Then quite suddenly I found myself at the entrance. I pushed forward not daring to stop and entered the cave calling out as I did so, my voice quavering with false bravado.

'Hello, anyone here?'

It was dark and cold but I noticed a small fire burning deeper inside and this did cast a bit of light, not much but enough to make out my surroundings. Though it had no effect whatsoever on the cold atmosphere. My eyes quickly adjusted to the dim light and I could see a small figure squatting by the fire.

At first I thought he was naked but then noticed a ragged loincloth around him. His hair was dirty and long, hanging, covering his face with twisted, matted strands. I approached closer to him and became aware of a low, muttered, mournful chant.

He threw something on the fire making it flare up. I called out in surprise and jumped back.

A cackling laugh broke from him.

I took the cassette recorder from my bag and with trembling fingers pressed the play button. Mamet's voice issued forth requesting what I needed. His soft lisp so comical before took on a more sinister hue. He seemed to be present even though I knew it came from the player. One desirable effect it had was to silence the kuncen.

After Mamet finished speaking, the kuncen stood up and proceeded to shuffle around me, peering up at me with his head to one side in a curious, bird-like and predatory way. His body was twisted and deformed and looked more animal than human. He stopped at one point and jabbed a finger towards the cassette player. I rewound the tape and pressed play again. Mamet's voice lost none of its menace the second time round. This time the kuncen bent low and placed the side of his head close to the machine but still squinted up at me from the ground.

'Do you understand?' I asked in English, like a fool.

He stared blankly at me. '

Mengerti kamus?' I repeated in Indonesian.

His mouth twisted into a black toothed grimace and a screech burst out of it as he spun around the cave. I held out the bag of offerings and he snatched it away and pulled out the contents one by one exclaiming with pleasure at each of them but the cockerel drew forth the biggest ululation of joy.

Abruptly, he picked up a burning stick out of the fire and drew three charcoal circles on the floor of the cave. One around me and two others spaced apart, they formed a triangle. From a shadowy recess he produced what looked like a knife and picking up the bound, black cockerel in one swift movement sliced its head from its body. Then to my horror upended the poor fowl and drank the gushing blood from its severed neck. Flinging the corpse from him, he looked wildly around the cave and finally at me. I truly thought he was going to leap and slice through my neck but then quite unexpectedly he bent down and picked up the scattered flowers and almost tenderly placed them in one of the two remaining circles. He started jabbing with claw like fingers towards me. He came closer and it was all I could do to not move away. The stench from him was awful and ripped at my throat like acid fumes. He was grunting and continued to point at my chest then he touched my shirt pocket and froze, unmoving as a statue. His eyes looked into mine and I was startled to see intelligence in them, albeit an unhinged one. My fingers moved to my pocket by their own volition with no impulse from me and took the photograph of my nephew out. He sighed, a rasping sound of escaping air and pointed to the circle with the flowers. I understood and almost reverently moved and placed Simon's photo on the bed of flowers.

'Goodbye dear boy,' I quietly said to his picture, 'Have a full and wonderful life, remember me with fondness.' I moved back to my circle and waited for god knows what. The kuncen turned and leapt like a cat into the third circle.

A moan came from deep within him and ended in a rapid, manic chant that grew in intensity and volume. The louder it got the higher the flames of the fire seemed to dance. Now fear clutched at my heart. I became mesmerized by the flames and my horror grew deeper as the shapes they made grew recognizable. I saw creatures of such monstrosity, devils with horns and souls in torment, writhing in agony. Then suddenly one of the shapes moved out of the fire.

It was a beast of such horrendous appearance, a nightmare vision that not even Hieronymus Bosch could have imagined or created.

The presence of this ghastly hell spawn caused the kuncen to whirl like a demented dervish within his circle screaming at the top of his voice. Then he dropped to the ground in supplication to the creature, his face to the floor. The beast approached the kuncen and gently fondled the filthy locks of his hair.

Up to this point I had watched with rising panic all that had taken place. A growing awareness that what I had done was wrong, so very wrong took hold of me. Then came the moment when I felt my heart freeze with fear as if a claw of the demon had pierced it. The creature turned, looked at me, raised an arm and beckoned with a talon. I was helpless and felt my feet shuffle towards it, I desperately tried to stop them but had no control. I drew ever closer to the foul monster. The creature's eyes held mine, pulling me toward it. I strained with every sinew of my body to resist it until the sweat ran in rivulets down my face. I tried to raise my hands to cover my eyes but they would not move.

'Stop'. A loud commanding voice split the air. I felt the hypnotic hold over me wane and the demon turned with fury to face the intruder.

I managed to take a step back and also turned to look.

'Mamet?' But not the Mamet I knew. I could palpably feel the power emanating from him. Beams of energy poured forth from his hands and wrapped themselves around the demon who twisted and tore at them with his claws. The demon broke one arm free and I could see that soon it would be able to move. Mamet raised his arms and in a mighty voice called out in a language I could not recognise. The energy from his hands intensified, if that was possible, causing the demon to shrink away in agony. Then roaring in frustration it spun back to the fire, snatching up the kuncen on the way and breaking his back with one casual twist of its talons before disappearing into the flames with its prey.

Neither Mamet nor I moved for a while. Mamet was the first. He came towards me and looked me in the eyes with that humourless, twist to his lips that passed for a smile.

'Well Mr Peters that was a close shave, a very close shave indeed.'

All of a sudden I was incandescent with rage. 'What... Why are you here? What the hell do you think you are doing?' I ran and picked up Simon's photograph. An image flashed in my mind of Mamet standing all-powerful as the energy flashed from his hands and enveloped the...the... 'What was that thing?'

'That was a demon summoned by the kuncen.'

'Oh my god. It came for me' I yelled angrily at him, 'What will happen to Simon now?'

'Calm down Mr Peters the spell will be completed. Your nephew will live and you will not have to sacrifice your life as the kuncen has paid with his,' he giggled in a girlish, high falsetto way, 'Quite ironic really, don't you think Mr. Peters?' I stared in silent bewilderment at him.

'No?' he giggled again, 'I thought you British pride yourselves on being masters of irony. As to why I'm here well that is purely to do with my own vanity. My powers have been steadily increasing and your coming to see me gave an opportunity to test them against a worthy opponent. They don't come more worthy than a demon from the pits of hell.'

'Good God Mamet do you mean you used me as bait to play your hellish games?'

He shrugged in a dismissive way as if we were talking of no more than a spilt drink or a broken glass. *'Comme ci comme ca* as the French would say.'

Then his manner changed and he towered over me in a very threatening way. His quiet lisp became even more pronounced. 'You still have your life and for that I shall expect payment. What exactly? Well let me think about that, but let us say for the present that you belong to me. Now I will leave this place. You of course can leave and do what you wish for the time being, while I decide what to do with you.' Those last few words to me were said heavily and with menace. Then he giggled as he walked away throwing over his shoulder 'Unless of course you want to stay and become the next kuncen in residence.' I shuddered at the thought and hurried after his already retreating back, like a servant following his master.

As I followed him down the mountain I was afraid. What had he meant? How could I belong to him? But even as I thought that, I knew anything was possible with regard to Mamet. I had seen him battle and defeat a demon and knew his power was immense.

At the base he strode off without a word or a backward glance and for this I was grateful as the man scared the living daylights out of me.

Later that day while I was waiting at the nearest airport for my flight back home, my phone rang. It was Jennie and she was laughing.

'Jonathan I have great news, Simon has just had some tests and he's in remission, the cancer has completely disappeared. The doctors are astounded.'

I laughed with her. 'Wonderful news darling, I'll be there as soon as I can.'

'Where are you?'

'Oh, out of town, I had a little bit of business to attend to. See you all soon.'

I caught myself absentmindedly scratching my skin. The rash was spreading fast. Then it hit me and all fear of Mamet left me in an instant. I started to chuckle and soon was roaring with laughter to the bewilderment of the people sitting near me. You see I wasn't worried at all by what Mamet had said.

I'd been given the results of my skin tests a few days before climbing the mountain. Apparently, I had a particularly malignant melanoma. The doctor had given me no more than six months to a year to live. Every time I looked in the mirror I'd been reminded of the truth. I had told no one and kept the information to myself. Otherwise I would have had to face the cold reality of it.

What Mamet didn't know therefore, was that I was already a condemned man and a stronger force controlled me. God's summons took preference over whatever he held over me. Oh yes, I could appreciate irony just as well as the next man.

Mamet wanted a duel did he? Let him duel with God.

GO'IB

'Corporal!' The Colonel's voice barked out.
Immediately a soldier stepped into the room.

'Sir!' he replied snapping to attention.

'Ask Captain Ramli to come and see me,'
said Colonel Sudharto.

'Yes sir.' The corporal, saluted smartly
before leaving the room.

Colonel Sudharto nodded in appreciation
of the discipline he saw in his men. It was
Captain Ramli's vigorous training, that kept the
men up to scratch. The man might be a bit of a
pedant when it came to rules and regulations
but by Allah it was needed.

The army was dispersed in isolated units
all over Indonesia and they were running what
was virtually a guerrilla operation against the

hated Dutch. Colonel Sudharto's lips set in a grim line. The war against the Japanese had finally ended and then the Dutch had just walked back in and taken over. The Indonesian army as such was in a terrible state, scattered and out of touch. Discipline in such a situation was apt to become a bit sloppy and in some units very lax indeed but not in his. Ramli might be a hardnosed, humourless individual but there was no questioning his devotion to his country and his almost obsessive desire for freedom.

The Colonel liked Ramli. He recognised a kindred spirit in the man. That was why they were soldiers. They were fighting for the blood of their country. He looked over at the flag hanging in the corner of his makeshift office, the red and white stripes reminding him of the blood that had already been shed and the white of the spiritual purity of people and their mission. He gazed thoughtfully at the envelopes on the table in front of him. Very ordinary looking white envelopes but they contained information that was vital to their struggle. Information about Dutch troop movements and positions but more importantly, information about the groundswell of the kampung soldiers. The farmers, the villagers, the very lifeblood of Indonesia. They were gathering, uniting, they were rising in anger. It was information that must be taken from where they were in Cirebon across the mountains to Bogor, a distance of eight hundred or so kilometres, through the jungle, travelling from kampung to kampung.

'You never told me what happened to you in the jungle that time the Colonel sent you to Bogor,' said Aii. He poured the hot water onto the coffee heaped in the bottom of the cup and spooned in the sugar making it strong and sweet, just like his friend Ramli liked it. Ramli took the cup from Aii and blew meditatively on the surface watching the coffee grounds settle on the bottom. Aii waited for his friend to speak. It was no use hurrying Ramli; he was a man of few words and did things in his own time.

'I have told very few people,' said Ramli eventually. 'Would you say I was a crazy man, someone who tells stories, someone full of empty air?'

Aii snorted in amusement, 'Just the opposite my friend, why?'

Ramli sipped his coffee. 'If another man told me what I'm going to tell you, I would say he was a bull-shitter,' replied Ramli. 'It started from the moment the Colonel sent for me. I was preparing to go to see my family in Jakarta and if I remember correctly had even packed my bag.

I thought nothing of the summons at the time I just presumed the Colonel wanted to wish me a safe journey and perhaps pass on a few messages. I went to his office and knocked on the door. 'Enter,' the colonel called out. I went into the room and stood to attention.

'At ease Captain, sit down.' The colonel indicated a chair opposite the table. I sat.

'I have a job for you, a very important job,' said the Colonel.

Inwardly I sighed. Bang goes my trip to Jakarta I thought but outwardly my awareness perceptibly heightened. If it was possible to come to attention sitting in a chair, I did so then.

'Captain Ramli, these envelopes,' the Colonel indicated those in front of him, 'contain information of the utmost importance to General Sudarsono who is, as far as I know, in Bogor at this moment. I want you to take them to him. This information must not fall into Dutch hands.'

I nodded. I knew what was being asked of me - if I was captured by the Dutch, then certain torture and if I was lucky welcome death would be my reward.

At this time in Indonesia, there were a few roads linking cities. Between small towns and villages were paths which a bicycle or maybe a horse and cart could negotiate. Mentally a section of my mind was already planning my route. Uncannily as if knowing what I was thinking, the Colonel continued. 'You'll have to avoid all known routes to Bogor, small or otherwise. We've received information that the enemy know about these documents.

As a result they have flooded the area from here to Bogor with troops. In fact worse than that, we believe that Captain Westerling of the Dutch KNIL detachment has been sent from Sulawesi to head the operation.'

That did worry me as we had received disturbing reports of atrocities committed by Westerling on children and hospital patients.

'You'll have to go across the mountains through the jungle,' the Colonel continued. 'That is why I'm sending just you with no back up force. More than one man will attract attention and if someone is passing on information, you'll have a better chance if only you and I know you have the documents. I'm sorry about your leave to Jakarta but that's one of the reasons why I'm sending you. If we do have a traitor amongst us then your trip to Jakarta will be the perfect blind. Speed is vital; the sooner General Sudarsono gets this information the better. He must have this information at the very outside, not more than two weeks from now, ten days would be better.'

I showed no reaction to what my Colonel said. I just nodded, but inside my head I was thinking - eight hundred kilometres in ten days, through the jungle, is he mad?

Colonel Sudharto smiled across at me. 'I

don't want you to go. I need you too much here, but you're the best I've got and the best chance of this information getting through on time. Leave as soon as possible, this afternoon if you can. Right that's all Captain Ramli. Except good luck and may Allah go with you.'

As he was saying this, the Colonel put the envelopes into a pouch and handed them over.

I took them and saluted.

'I'll do my best sir,' I said and left the room.

I slipped away that afternoon, quietly and without fuss. A small kit bag slung over my shoulder contained food and water and a folded ground sheet was strapped to the side. A few people saw me leave and asked where I was going. I shouted over my shoulder some garbled reply about going to Jakarta on a family visit. You lucky so and so they said. I smiled and thought yes a lucky so and so. I checked my compass for the right direction and then the jungle swallowed me up.

It's a strange place, the jungle. Many people don't like it, they're afraid of it but it doesn't bother me. I have time to think. I like the cool shade of the trees - the sun cannot reach you there. It's another world, not our world - a world of snakes, of spiders, big spiders, of birds with many colours and their beautiful songs, of tigers and insects. This is their world and I respect it. I don't try and fight it, it's bigger than me. I try to accept it and flow with it and so it lets me be.

My clothes were soon wet with sweat as I cut my way forward. The jungle was not thick and I moved quickly through it. I travelled for many hours stopping only for food, water and to check my direction. When night came I stopped and put my groundsheet down to rest awhile. I slept deeply and woke a couple of hours later. The moon was up and it was very bright, there was enough light filtering through the trees to see my way so I decided to carry on. I was slower but still making good speed. I continued like this for a couple of days and began to think that I had a chance of making it to Bogor on time.

Physically I was in very good shape. The previous couple of months I had been training the men very hard in the jungle so everything was familiar to me. I did not feel tired and was full of energy. My food was running low so I kept an eye out for snakes to catch. There were also many cassava plants along the way, the roots of which I could easily dig out. I saw banana and papaya trees with lots of fruit so I wasn't worried about going hungry.

It was during the third day that I caught the smell of wood smoke and knew that I must be near a small Kampung. It seemed to be coming from the direction I was going as it got stronger the further I went. Then rising over a small hill I saw the Kampung. It was across the valley scattered over the side of the next hill. There were about a dozen small bamboo huts. I slipped down into the valley and climbed up the other side. The children saw me first and ran calling to their parents. I waited until the men came towards me then I smiled and called out a greeting. They smiled back and beckoned me up greeting me. I sighed with relief. I wasn't afraid but sometimes the hill people can be very suspicious and not very welcoming. They shared their food with me, just roots and boiled leaves of the cassava plant. But I was hungry and I was grateful. I asked them about the Dutch soldiers but they hadn't seen any and then I warned them to be careful as they might be in that area. They gave me water and food to take with me. I felt moved by their simple hospitality.

I travelled far that day and slept that night when it got dark. As before I woke refreshed after a couple of hours. Again the moon was bright and there was enough light to see my way. I thanked Allah for his blessing, folded my groundsheet, drank some water and then started off, slipping easily into a rhythm of movement that had me flowing through the jungle.

Daylight came as I emerged from a patch of dense jungle. It had been hard work moving through it. Thorns had snagged my trousers and shirt in several places and I was bleeding from numerous small scratches. My pace had slowed right down and I knew I had to pick it up to realistically get to Bogor on time. But I was tired, so I decided to rest a short while. I sat with my back against a tree and mentally sent a message of relaxation to my muscles. Soon I felt the tiredness begin to ease itself out of my body while idly scanning the way I had come. I had been travelling upward for some time and now found myself perched on top of a small mountain. The cool morning breeze was a blessing after the oppressive heat of the thick jungle I had just been through. I was pleased with the distance I had travelled over the past few days. Mountains and hills stretched away into the distance all covered with jungle. Mist and cloud clung and spread itself over the mountain tops like the kapok stuffing from a mattress, slicing off the tops making mountain tables for Allah to feast off. My heart ached for the beauty of my country.

I noticed smoke spiralling up from a distant hill. I was puzzled as it was too much to be cooking fires. Then with a growing sense of horror I realised it was coming from the small village that had fed me. The smoke could only mean one thing, Dutch soldiers!

They were burning the huts of the village.

That meant they probably knew about me. I couldn't rely on the villagers not to tell them especially if lives were threatened. But why had the soldiers set fire to their homes? Rage flooded through me at the sadistic destruction and senseless waste of it all. I now felt more determined than ever to get the information to Bogor on time. I stood up all tiredness banished and checked my compass. I looked once more at the billowing smoke and let my fury fill me with energy, then I set off once more at a fast pace.

That was my mistake. I was moving too quickly down the other side of the mountain and the ground I was on was covered with damp, loose leaves. Suddenly my feet slipped and I started to slither down a slope. I tried to dig my heels in but that just flipped me over and I found myself sliding face down. I grabbed what I could but there was nothing strong enough within reach to stop me. Then I went over the edge of a ravine. I was too surprised to be afraid. I bounced down the side, hitting rocks and small trees as I went.

Occasionally I managed to get hold of a branch or creeper which pulled me up with a jolt and then they were wrenched away again as I continued to fall. I remember my face passing centimetres from that of a startled monkey, one of those small ones with a black face and we both screeched with fright. Then I hit my head and passed out.

When I came to, I lay still and mentally checked my condition. I hurt, that was to be expected after a fall like the one I had just taken but nothing felt broken. Gently raising my right hand to my face, I winced with the pain. A jagged tear down my forearm had stopped bleeding but stung badly. My face was also cut and I had a lump the size of a chicken's egg on my head.

Miraculously these seemed to be my only injuries. I moved my legs and gingerly sat up then slowly got to my feet. A wave of nausea and dizziness almost had me passing out but I caught hold of a tree branch until the moment passed. My head began to throb unbearably. I fumbled for my water bottle, unscrewed it and with great effort as every movement that I took sent my bruised and battered body into a spasm of pain, I took a few swallows. The relief was immediate. I had to stop myself from gulping it all down. Carefully I sipped at the water. I sparingly poured some into the palm of my left hand and bathed my face with my handkerchief. Then I cleaned my arm. After I had cleaned the blood away, I looked at the wound on my arm and knew that I had to sterilize it soon before problems set in.

I forced myself to slowly scour the area around me for something I could use. I was in luck! I found a cacabean plant. I cut a handful of leaves with my Kris and using the handle I crushed them into a poultice against a stone. I gently applied this to the lump on my head, my face and my arm. I wrapped a bandana around my head and face to hold it in place and tied a banana leaf around my arm. Then I sank to the ground completely exhausted.

I was dazed and in a lot of pain but I knew I had to keep moving. If I rested too long stiffness would set in and then I would be in even more trouble. I allowed myself about half an hour then pulled my body wearily to my feet.

'Brengsek! Brengsek! Brengsek!' I remember cursing out aloud when I found that my compass was smashed and completely unworkable. I had no idea which direction to go but forced myself to move. I stumbled off blindly, wracked with pain and my head thudding with each step I took. For all I knew I might be heading straight for the Dutch soldiers. I have never felt more depressed and miserable.

Unbelievably I found what seemed to be a path. Maybe some animal had walked that way, I don't know. I was too tired and in too much pain to worry about what animal it was, if indeed it was an animal that had made the path. I just followed it in relief as a direction to go, to give me purpose and not just blunder about in a rising panic. The way came to an enormous bush about the height of two men and maybe five or so metres across. Its leaves were dark green and glossy and it was covered in small, white flowers.

It was a wonderful bush and the sweet scent from the flowers filled the air around me, lifting me up and easing my throbbing head. Then I found myself standing in front of it. I looked left and right, there was no path! I looked down at my feet and behind me, there was the path.

Whatever had come that way had gone straight through the bush but iit was too thick and dense to go through and it was intact without any breakage. With my mind reeling from this latest confusing thought, I turned and walked around it and to my astonishment I found a sheep.

It had no right to be there, sheep belonged on farms not in the middle of the jungle. I had the distinct impression that it was waiting for me. It looked at me and then turned and walked away. I watched it go. It only went a few steps and then snorted impatiently and turned back to look at me again.

I felt a strong compulsion to follow it. It seemed to be beckoning to me. Its eyes held mine. It spoke to me, I don't mean words came out of its mouth but I heard the words in my head. You see that is why I haven't told people about this. Was it something I imagined? Was the knock on my head more serious than I thought? It looked just like a sheep but it wasn't a sheep. A sheep is just a sheep. It is a good animal, a useful animal but a stupid animal. This sheep was not stupid. I saw the Universe in its eyes, the planets and the stars. I saw love and compassion, understanding and knowledge. When it looked into my eyes, I felt naked before it. I felt as though it saw into the very depths of me and there was nothing, nothing about me that was not revealed to it. It turned again and walked away and this time I followed.

Up and down mountains, across rivers and through rice fields, I followed the sheep. We moved quickly and steadily. I soon walked off my aches and pains and found to my surprise that I had plenty of energy. The sheep led the way and I followed trotting along behind.

Amazingly the terrain we covered wasn't difficult. It was as though the jungle made way for us. I say for us but really I mean for the sheep. At times I felt my sense of reality slipping and caught myself talking to the sheep. I don't mean we had a conversation like you or I would, a sheep can't talk but it did communicate with me. I would formulate a question in my mind and before I had finished, the answer would be there in my thoughts.

Absurd isn't it? But it happened. Sometimes the answer would be another question and so it went on. If we passed people working in the rice fields I would stop and talk and the sheep would wait patiently until we had finished. Nobody commented on the sheep, it was as though they didn't see it. But it was real, it was solid. I didn't imagine it. I know this because I touched it and felt it. I felt its coat, the soft roughness of its wool and when we slept, we slept close together for company.

I had no worries about getting to Bogor in time to give the letters to General Sudarsono; the ground seemed to flow under our feet. It seemed as if everything in the Universe was focussed on our mission.

'It is,' said the sheep's voice in my head.

'How can this be?' I asked.

'Because you are focussed.'

'Who are you?' I asked.

'I am you,' was the reply. I am a sheep? I thought in confusion.

'Yes you are a sheep, you are all sheep. You are the Garuda bird flying above us.'

I looked up and yes there it was a speck in the sky above us. An eagle flying guard over us, its sentinel eyes ever watchful.

The voice in my head spoke again. 'You are

the grass beneath your feet and the worms in the ground. You are everything and everything is you.'

I stopped walking at this and the sheep stopped too waiting patiently again.

'I do not understand,' I said.

'I know,' said the sheep. Patiently, as if speaking to a small child it continued. 'Everything in the Universe is connected because we all come from the same energy source. You are energy and so is that mosquito,' it said as I slapped the insect on my arm.

'But the mosquito is bad. It sucks my blood and gives me fever.'

'It is also food for other insects and animals,' the sheep said. 'Energy does not judge, it just is.'

I stood confused and I swear to you the sheep smiled at me.

'Imagine an energy source so vast it has no edge, no measurement. Every thought from every living being, every atom, creates more energy connected to the mother energy. Specks of energy, some huge in size like a planet and some so small you cannot see them even with your microscopes.'

I couldn't imagine it and said so.

'I know,' said the sheep.

'What about Allah,' I asked, '

Allah created everything. Did he create this source energy?'

There was a long pause while the sheep looked at me unblinkingly. 'Allah is a thought, Allah is energy,' it said eventually.

'Are you saying Allah is not real?' I doggedly questioned it, worrying at this thought.

'Allah is a thought, Allah is energy,' it repeated.

'No!' I said angrily, 'I cannot accept this.'

'I know but it doesn't matter.' The sheep turned. 'Now come we must go. The Universe may be working for you but you must help it.'

The sheep trotted off and I followed, a very confused man. We continued our journey and every day was the same. More questions from me and the same infuriating, confusing answers from the sheep.

The first night of our journey together when we stopped for a rest, I took the cloth from my head and the banana leaf from my arm to check my wounds; the sheep came up and looked with me. Its face was close to mine and I smelt its breath. It was sweet and scented like the bush with the white flowers.

A voice in my head said, 'Let me clean them for you.'

Then the sheep leant forward and licked

my arm. I pulled away in surprise but then I realised the relief to my arm was immediate. Nervously I offered my arm to it again and stared in wonder as the skin closed over the wound. I sat quietly while the sheep did the same to the cuts on my head and face. Again the relief was instantaneous. It was at this point I thought I might be going mad.

'No, you are not losing your mind,' the voice spoke again. 'Just experiencing the unknown.'

We reached the outskirts of Bogor on the tenth day after I left Cirebon. I was not surprised. By now if I had flapped my arms like a bird and floated over the ground I would have considered it to be an everyday occurrence. I stood on a rise looking at the buildings below bathed with the golden glow of the setting sun.

I remember thinking how wonderful life is. I looked around for the sheep to thank it but it had vanished. I also remember thinking what a fool I was. Such is the logical aspect of my mind I was already beginning to doubt that it had ever existed and was putting the whole experience together logically as a result of the knock on my head.

But then I noticed my hand was clutching a tuft of sheep's wool. I looked at my arm and saw the thin white line of healed scar tissue. I felt such an overpowering rush of awe I staggered under the weight of it.

I made contact with Sudarsono's men and they took me immediately to see the General. I handed over the pouch of letters with a sense of relief. He opened them in front of me and scanned the contents, a smile growing on his face as he read them. He looked up at me,

'Well done Captain Ramli, this is excellent news. Very, very good news. Now get some food and some rest.' He paused for a second then added with a smile, 'But first have a bath.'

I grinned back, 'Yes sir.'

Ramli stopped talking and stared into the remains of his cold coffee. It was the most Aii had ever heard him speak since he had known him.

After a while Aii spoke.

'You say the sheep just disappeared. What do you mean?'

'I don't know,' Ramli looked at him. 'I don't know what to think. Did I imagine the whole thing or was it really…' his voice trailed off.

'A Go'ib' said Aii softly, awe creeping into his voice.

'Yes,' said Ramli, 'A Go'ib.'

They both fell silent at this thought. A Go'ib. A sheep but not a sheep, a lamb of God, a messenger from Allah, an angel, call it what you will.

'You know,' said Ramli eventually, 'I did have a nasty fall and knock on the head and would be quite happy to say I imagined it all, except for one thing.'

'Oh what's that?' asked Aii.

Ramli dug in his pocket, pulled out a small tin and handed it to his friend. Aii opened the tin and looked inside then very slowly and reverently he reached inside and held up a tuft of wool. Aii looked across at his friend and Ramli nodded back. A slight breeze started up making the wool flutter like the fragile wings of a butterfly. Aii dropped the wool back into the tin as though it were alive, quickly replaced the lid and handed the tin back to Ramli. They didn't speak for a while after that and Ramli noticed that his friend seemed uncomfortable, almost afraid.

He sighed, was it always going to be like this? He felt as though a key had turned, a door had opened but only he could see into the room. He made some excuse and left.

Ramli walked down the street in Jakarta and people passed him, wait they didn't pass, they flowed around him. What was the word? Energy! Yes that was it, energy. We are all specks of energy, Ramli thought. He flowed down the street with them not knowing where he was going. But that did not matter anymore.

FLOTSAM

I wake from a troubled sleep. Images of my family have fractured the welcome coma of night. I try not to think about my wife and child. The memories they evoke are unbearable and too painful. During the days I push my consciousness deep within my mind and shut down my feelings. But I have no control over my dreams. I pray for a release from the awfulness of this life. But it never comes. When I sleep at night, my one thought before the dark of sleep comes and takes me is that I will not wake. Then it would be over. But the freedom never comes.

My name is Najib Abdullah. I am from Afghanistan. I am forty five years old, My life is dead. Help me please.

I rise from the stone floor of my cell and

stand for a few moments. My mind is heavy and sluggish. I move to the basin of water in the corner of my cell and splash water on my face, a ritual of cleansing and a habitual daily action. While doing this, my mind unwittingly and unwontedly steps back to a time before.

'Naji,' says my wife as she looks critically at her face in the bathroom mirror. It always amuses me at the way she crinkles up her eyes and pouts her lips coquettishly. She turns and examines herself sideways in the mirror, sucking in her stomach. God how I love her.

   'Naji,' says my wife again drawing my name out. I recognize that sound. It pre-empts a request that I won't be able to turn down and that I don't really want to do.

   'Yes,' I say cautiously.

   My wife, Nareem, continues. 'Mrs Gutra was asking about her daughter's wedding again. She really does want you to give her away; you know she has no husband.'

   I sigh. 'Yes, but hasn't she got brothers or uncles who can do that?'

   'She wants you Naji,' says my wife, a certain firmness coming into her voice. 'You are an important man and it would do her great honour if you gave her daughter away.'

   An important man I might be but I was

also rather a shy one. A public event such as the Gutra wedding would be a torment to me but there was no getting out of it. 'Ok. Tell her I'll do it.'

My wife comes over to me and hugs me, kissing me warmly. Her lips taste of cinnamon. 'You're such a dear.'

The phone rings, spoiling the moment. I groan.

'Mr Abdullah is that you sir?'

It is the voice of my assistant in the government department where I work.

'Yes?' I reply, a little tartly as it is my day off and I do not like being disturbed by work on my day off.

'We've had people here asking about you, sir.' There is some quality about my assistant's voice that worries me. I try to think what it is and then I recognise it. Fear, my assistant sounds very afraid.

'What people?'

'Taliban officials, sir.'

Just the sound of the name, *Taliban*, clutches at my stomach like a blow. 'They were very angry to find you not here; they said they will come tomorrow.'

I listen to what my assistant says with only half my concentration; my mind is reeling. The Taliban! And they were asking for me! You do not need to be a clever man to know that this is very dangerous. One can't reason with the Taliban, they are dogmatic fundamentalists. If they take it into their heads that I am guilty of some crime, then there is no appeal. My life is in danger.

'Thank you for the warning,' I say. 'It is good of you.'

'I'm very worried for you sir. What are you going to do?'

I mentally shrug. 'I don't know yet, I really don't know. Thank you for your concern. Listen you better hang up, the less you speak to me the better. In case I don't get a chance to contact you again, I just want to say thank you for all your hard work. You're a good man. Goodbye my friend.' Then I put the phone down.

When I go back into my living room, my wife is teaching our daughter, Attiqah, how to iron clothes. I stand and watch them for a while just absorbing the sheer, simple domesticity of it.

'So remember,' says my wife, 'when ironing shirts, iron them on the inside of the shirt and be careful of ironing over buttons.'

She looks up and smiles at me, raising her eyebrows in mock exasperation at Attiqah's efforts. Then she sees my face and knows that something is dreadfully wrong.

'Enough for today, Attiqah. Go and play with your toys now, I want to talk with Daddy.'

Attiqah jumps up and kisses her mother and then runs to me, she takes my hand and touches it to her forehead before running out of the room.

'What is it?' Nareem asks.

'The Taliban,' I say, 'they've been asking for me at my office.' I see my fear reflected in her eyes.

'Why?'

'That's just it, I don't know. It could be for anything. My name, the fact that I was head of the Olympic committee, some jealous person reporting me for some minor misdemeanour, I don't know. They will come again to my office tomorrow.'

'Right,' my wife says. 'You must go and you must hide.'

'Go where Nareem?' I cry. 'Hide where? There is nowhere safe from the Taliban in this country.'

'Then you must go to another country.'

I look at her with surprise.

'What? What are you saying? I cannot leave you and Attiqah. The Taliban will come here.'

'I know,' she says. 'And I will curse you and revile you. I will say you ran away like a thief in the night, without a word, leaving me nothing. Like all men you proved yourself to be a worthless shit. When you find the bastard, I will say to them, tell me as I want to be the first one to spit in his false face.'

My mouth drops open in amazement. Then she grins broadly.

'You see,' she says. 'Even you believe me.' I start to chuckle then.

'I've never heard you speak like that before,' I say.

'There are a lot of things about me that would surprise you,' she says.

My eyes widen.

'Come, we must decide where you will go. We must get money today and I have gold you can take. Your position means you will have no problem getting an air ticket and leaving the country but you must go today before a block is put on you.'

'But where shall I go?'

We both think for a minute.

'Singapore,' says Nareem finally. 'There will be no problem entering and once there you can decide what to do.'

'Why don't you and Attiqah come with me?' I ask.

'No,' says Nareem. 'You must go today and alone. There are many things that must be completed before I can join you. I will go to my family in the south and wait for your call.'

'But our home is here, this is our country.'

'Our home here is finished,' Nareem interrupts me with a great deal of force and bitterness. 'Forget our home in Afghanistan; we will make a new home in a new country.'

I look at my wife with admiration. 'You are magnificent. I knew there was a reason I married you.'

Nareem bursts out laughing and then suddenly bursts into tears. She throws her arms around me and kisses me passionately. Then she laughs again.

'You crazy man,' she says. 'Now let's call Attiqah, she must be told what is going to happen. She has a part to play too.'

So my surreal departure from Afghanistan begins. Both of us are amazed at how coolly Attiqah accepts the situation.

'Wow, like a movie,' she says.

She becomes little miss actress learning her lines well.

I go to the airport alone as it is too dangerous for Nareem to go with me, in case anyone sees her. When my plane finally takes off the relief floods through me to be followed by the deepest and darkest sorrow I have ever felt to be leaving my family behind.

Singapore is a confusing morass of loneliness. Then I meet Sadiq, a fellow countryman, a welcome face in a strange and foreign land.

'I will help you,' he says. 'We will go to Indonesia and I will get you the necessary visas for Australia.'

I am excited. Australia will be our new home, our new country. I will send for Nareem and Attiqah and we will make a new life there.

Sadiq and I enter Indonesia easily, buying tourist visas at Jakarta airport. Sadiq takes me to a hotel in a place called Jalan Jaksa. I stay mostly in my room, only leaving it to eat in the hotel café or watch the television there. I did go out into the street the first night I was there and a young girl with a very short skirt and an uncovered head asked me for sex. I was shocked and embarrassed and quickly fled back to my room. Sadiq asks me for five thousand US dollars to make the visas. It is most of the money I have left. I pay it. I will soon earn more in Australia.

Then the nightmare starts. We go to the airport and I am stopped at immigration. Suddenly Sadiq is not there, he disappears. I am taken to Karentina Kalideres Immigration prison. I am beaten many times by the Burmese trustees and frequently cursed and slapped by the Indonesian guards after they take what little money I have left. When I have no more money, the guards lose interest in me. For that I am grateful. I am also grateful that the Afghanistan Embassy are not informed about me and make no attempt to contact me. If I am deported, I will return to a death sentence. A living hell stretches bleakly before me. So it continues, a year or more. I lose track of time.

I come to from the memory of my wife and daughter and the grief is almost too much to take.

There is the clunk of keys turning in my cell door as it is unlocked for the daily exercise time in the yard.

I stagger out into the bright sunshine, a welcome distraction from the darkness of my cell and gratefully slump down to the ground and let the sun warm my skin.

'Hey you, Najib.'

A voice cuts through my thoughts and a shadow falls over me. I look up at one of the guards standing in front of me. He gestures brusquely at me and I automatically flinch away from the blow that doesn't come. He laughs.

'Get up dog, come with me.' The guard turns and walks away.

I stumble to my feet and follow. What now I think? But I know better than to ask.

I am taken to a long room with plastic tables and chairs.

'Sit there.' The guard points to a chair. Then he leaves.

I look around the room. Why am I here? Maybe an embassy official has come to see me? Oh God I pray not, that would mean deportation and the Taliban.

'Father!'

I turn incredulously at the sound and see my daughter running towards me with her arms stretched out. Behind her comes Nareem with a huge smile on her face and tears streaming down her cheeks. Next to her is a middle-aged Chinese woman. I jump up and find Attiqah's arms around me. Then Nareem is there and the three of us become one hugging beast of happiness.

Later sitting at the table, holding Nareem and Attiqah's hands, I sit in a state of stupefied wonder as I listen to my wife's explanation of this miracle. The Chinese woman is Mrs Lee a representative from the United Nation's High Commission for Refugees and she has arranged refugee status for us in Australia. It has been difficult but my Olympic connections have tipped the balance in my favour. Nareem traced me from Singapore to the prison in Jakarta and has bribed the immigration officials to release me later that day.

I keep stroking their hands to convince me that they are really there.

'Today?' I can leave here today?'

'Yes today darling,' says Nareem. 'We fly tonight, to Australia, to our new home.'

I feel my heart will burst with joy.

EXOTIC FRUIT

The cocktail of traffic fumes, toxic factory waste and thick, acrid smoke caused by the general public's indiscriminate burning of household waste, hung heavy over the city. The billboard posters advertising, 'CLEAN AIR & BLUE SKIES', were mocked by the oily stains of pollution that marked them.

The posters puzzled me as I strolled through the rubbish-strewn streets to my next appointment. My name is Sam, Sam Spendlove and I sell insurance. Not very exciting, is it? I'm not a secret agent, a TV chef, or a porn star, but I'm quite good at selling insurance. I make a reasonable living and, as I have to traipse around from client to client chasing leads. I tend to notice my environment.

I'd given up using my car in the city of

Jakarta, northern Java. The antiquated road infrastructure coupled with the ever-increasing volume of traffic meant hours of frustration and a frayed temper. Also, it was on credit and the payments were getting a bit hard to find every month. I now preferred to walk; at least I got some exercise. Walking quite often took me less time than using my car and I was discovering areas of the city that I never knew existed by using little cuts and alleyways between buildings. Also there was always a little frisson of excitement as I dived down some gap in search of a shorter route. There was an element of risk but I am a big man and my size would put off any muggers. Besides which, I had always had a penchant for the seedier aspects of life and some of the areas I passed through were definitely seedy. They smelled different. Not just the garbage or the stale urine, it was the smell of the unknown and I like the unknown, the loaded glance of invitation and promise.

Did the posters mean that the city had blue skies and clean air? Were they meant to be a statement of fact? If so whoever had thought up the idea had not looked at the sky recently or taken in a good lungful. Perhaps the posters were meant to induce the power of positive thought, a mantra for people to hold onto. Or were they a kind of hopeless longing, a desperate desire?

'Meester! Meester!' A little girl with snot running down to her lips cut into my thoughts. She was waving a stick with a couple of bits of tin pushed on to it. When she shook it, it made a sort of ching-ching noise as the bits of tin rattled together like a distant cousin of the tambourine. She accompanied this with a toneless wail which if you were feeling kind you could say was singing.

Good grief, I thought, she can't be more than four years old. I dug in my pocket and pulled out some coins which I tossed into the plastic cup she was waving at me. She turned and ran off immediately. Probably straight to her boss.

It is a well-known fact that the child beggars are organised and controlled by some bastard who would beat the shit out of them if they didn't bring in their daily quota. Don't give to them; someone had once said to me, you just perpetuate the system. But when some bedraggled, half-starved, stunted child looked at you with that expressionless, old, old face that a child shouldn't have, you gave.

I could see a phalanx of child beggars converging on me, vampires swarming on to a plump, young virgin. To avoid them I shot down a passage between two shops.

It was barely big enough to accommodate my shoulders and I just prayed it wasn't going to be a dead end. It started to widen a little bit which raised my hopes and then 'sod's law' kicked in. The passage ended abruptly in a wire fence which curved over at the top and was strung with barbed wire. There was a metal gate set in the middle that was locked with a chain and padlock. I was just steeling myself for the humiliating return to the street and hoping against hope that the beggars had moved on when to my astonishment a heavily made up woman somewhere in her fifties, shuffled up to the gate, unlocked it, and held it open for me. Her age was a complete guess as the foundation, blusher and mascara were so thickly plastered on her face she could have been anywhere between forty and seventy.

Now what would you have done, be honest? Would you have politely declined and walked back to the street? Or would you have stepped through the gate like I did? Even when the gate shut behind me with a clanging finality that would have disturbed me in any other circumstance, I didn't give it a thought. I walked forward not knowing what to expect. It was as if they were expecting somebody to turn up, and I had, so they let me in. The alleyway turned a sharp right and then incredibly from a dark, dank passageway I found myself in the most beautiful garden. The woman who had opened the gate disappeared down a path to the left, leaving me alone.

The scent of jasmine and orange blossom hung heavy in the air. There were willows, cherry blossom, lemon and orange trees and jasmine everywhere. I was astounded and enchanted. It truly was an oasis amidst the smut and grime of Jakarta. The central feature was a fountain, a statue of a beautiful oriental woman pouring water from a jug. What made this statue different especially for Indonesia was her nudity.

She had beautiful breasts, small but proud with erect nipples. Her hair was long and she was smiling. She was raised up on her toes which gave her a very erotic look. The water fell musically into a pond. I was drawn towards it and saw it was covered with enormous water lilies; the leaves were several feet in diameter and gold, orange, red and black koi carp peered up at me from beneath them.

'We believe the koi are a symbol of strength, of wealth and a long life,' a voice spoke behind my left shoulder.

I turned, startled, to see a small man, Chinese, dressed in a simple black, silk tunic and leggings.

'I like them,' I replied. 'They always look so sure of themselves and just a little bit cantankerous. Their size is imposing too.'

He smiled up at me. 'Some people might find your size imposing.'

I laughed, 'Do you?'

He shook his head. 'No, I see no violence in you.'

What a curious thing to say, I thought but left it at that. 'Is this beautiful garden yours?' I asked looking around me, 'It's totally unexpected.'

'So are you,' he replied with a smile.

His answer suddenly made me feel uncomfortable, like I was a trespasser. He must have read my face because he opened his arms and said, 'Please, you are most welcome. Come inside and have some refreshment.' Then he abruptly started walking to one of the buildings that surrounded the courtyard.

Why not, I thought glancing at my watch; I have time before my next appointment. So I followed him and was soon sitting on a large raffia chair strewn with silk cushions. A ceiling fan created a welcome breeze in the large comfortable room. There was an ancient and beautiful rug hanging on one of the walls.

The scene on the rug was of cormorants diving for fish while their owners waited still as statues in the boats. I recognised the mists drifting over the water and rocky hills as being a typical view of Guilin in China. The mountains of the moon the area was known as. On the other walls I noticed a couple of sunflower paintings by Rukmini but the most magnificent piece was a large oil painting by Sunaryo, over two metres square. It was of courtesans and dancers applying their makeup. I recognised all the art as being of the highest quality and worth a lot of money. Some of my clients are extremely wealthy and insure their collections with me so I know what's what. I decided to leave my business card when I left, you never know.

I was impressed with the opulence and the taste. I half expected my host to clap his hands to bring servants scurrying to serve us. He didn't need to. No sooner were we settled when three beautiful women dressed in the Sundanese kabaya national costume came into the room, carrying trays of sliced fruit on ice and jugs of fresh strawberry and lemon juice. One of them, her hair pulled up and fixed with a clasp, showing off her exquisite neck, bent forward and placed a glass on a batik coaster in front of me. She looked up and her almond eyes locked with mine. She blushed and then smiled. The three women bowed and then left the room. I drew in a huge breath and realised that the entire time the women were in the room I hadn't breathed.

A slight chuckle tore my attention back to the Chinese man. He was smiling at my obvious confusion. 'I can see you like my flowers,' he said.

'Your flowers?' I asked, puzzled.

'Yes, all my girls are like flowers to me. The one you like very much, she is called Lily. Beautiful, isn't she?'

I nodded in agreement; still in my vision were her eyes, her gentle smile and the glow of pink in her cheeks.

'Would you like to make love to her?'

'What!?' the word exploded out of me. I was so surprised that I sat looking at him with my mouth open. We stayed like this, silent; looking at each other, for what seemed a ridiculous length of time. He was still smiling at me and I found his smile most disconcerting.

'Is... is this a joke?'

'No, it's not a joke,' he replied still smiling. 'If I have offended you, then please forgive me. We will forget the whole incident ever happened. Juice?' he offered, leaning forward.

'Wait!' I exclaimed.

He paused, 'You don't want any juice?'

'No! I mean yes, I mean you haven't offended me.'

'Oh good,' he said and indicated the drinks. 'Do you still want something to drink?'

I nodded, my mind felt slightly unhinged. This whole afternoon was beginning to take on a surreal aspect.

'Lemon or strawberry?' He looked at me.

'Strawberry please.'

He picked up the jug and started to pour - 'I will leave you now,' he said, 'I'm sorry to go but I have a previous appointment that I can't postpone.'

I started to rise with him, 'Oh in that case I better leave.'

'No please stay and finish your drink. If you wish,' he looked directly at me, 'Lily will join you.'

I felt my throat and tongue go dry at the thought and knew that more than anything else in the world I wanted to be alone with Lilly.

'Yes.' My voice came out as a rasp. 'Yes, I wish.'

He stood up and walked to the door. Then he turned and looked at me. All smiles had vanished, his face was almost stern. 'Good. Enjoy your time with her.'

Then he was gone, leaving me with the curious feeling that a sentence had just been passed on me.

While waiting, I felt disturbingly light headed and apprehensive. Soon there was a slight tap on one of the two doors of the room and then Lilly entered. She looked stunningly beautiful. Her lips were full and bright scarlet, voluptuously exciting. I desperately wanted to taste them, to push my tongue between them. Her hair was still up which emphasised her grace and poise. She radiated a magical mixture of elegance and rampant sexuality. I almost growled.

She came over to me and I stood up, finding delightfully that she was taller than I expected. Her long wrap around batik skirt concealing either very long legs or very high heels. I reached out to her hungry for contact but she held her hand up to stop me.

She then turned and left the room beckoning me with her eyes to follow. Within a minute, we'd walked a short distance down a corridor and entered another room. This room was made for love. There was a large but simple four-poster bed draped with the finest of lace. The sheets were silk and a soft, pastel cream colour. The lighting was subdued, just several scented candles burning. There was a small round table in the corner with a couple of high backed wooden chairs and a Barli nude on one wall. A large mirror covered the other wall.

I took an instant to take all this in. I drew her towards me, I wanted to possess Lily; I wanted her body writhing against mine. My breathing was short and fast and I could feel the blood pounding in my ears. She gently shook her head and taking my hands from her, led me to the bed.

'Not yet' she said.

These were the first words I had heard her speak. I groaned in frustration but at the same time the delay heightened every nerve end in my body. She slowly took off my clothes. Every action choreographed with delicate precision.

I lay on the bed while she gracefully removed her clothes. I watched in fascination as her naked body was revealed, it was perfection. Finally she reached up and unfastened her hair clasp, allowing her long hair to tumble down. It was then, for a brief instant, I noticed a similarity between the sculpture in the fountain and her. Then she joined me on the bed.

Later, spent, almost unconscious, I was vaguely aware of Lily getting off the bed, the rustle of her clothing, the slight click of the door opening and closing and then I dozed off. I came to about half an hour later. I lay there for a while and tried to make sense of what had happened.

I had never experienced anything like that before, ever. I listened for sounds of movement, for voices but there was nothing. What was this strange place, a brothel? No I didn't think so. No mention had been made of money and I felt it would have been insulting to do so. So where was I? So far, on the walls, I had seen art worth about a quarter of a million dollars. I decided to see if I could find the Chinese man and get some answers to my questions. I dressed and opened the door to the room to find the woman who had originally unlocked the gate, standing outside, holding my brief case. She held it out to me and turned indicating that I should follow her. We were soon crossing the courtyard containing the fountain and before I knew what was happening, I was standing outside the locked gate with not a soul in sight.

I looked at my watch. Damn! I had missed my appointment. I hate unpunctuality in others and make it a point never to be late for anything myself. While fumbling for my phone, I walked back down the narrow passage and out onto the street. I phoned my client, apologised and made an appointment for the following day. I decided to go home but then on the spur of the moment walked around the entire block trying to find the front entrance to where I had been. There had to be one, that metal gate couldn't be the only way in. I walked around the block twice but didn't find anything that looked right. There were several alleyways but they didn't lead anywhere. The buildings were all shop fronts and there were no private houses.

I tried to judge the area where it might be and went into those shops and made a few enquiries but to no avail. There were lots of Chinese Indonesians in that area, so it was a bit like asking if anyone knew of a Chinaman in Beijing. I gave up, called it a day and went home. I almost got run over twice because I wasn't concentrating. I kept thinking about Lily.

All night I thought of her and slept very badly. The next morning I spent doing the paper work that I do every morning and after lunch prepared to go to my appointments. On the way to the one I had missed the day before I passed the same passage and without hesitation, I went down it. I knew it would make me late. I knew it was an insane thing to do but I just had to do it. The part of my brain that censors stupid behaviour had switched off. My legs moved without paying any heed to instructions.

The same woman as yesterday was sitting on a stool as if expecting me. As soon as she saw me, she opened the gate and I walked in. After locking it behind me, she led the way across the courtyard and into the same building as before. Without hesitation she went down the corridor and tapped on the door of the room. 'Masuk' said a voice. She opened the door and I went in, I heard the door close behind me. Sitting on one of the chairs at the table was Lily; she stood up and came towards me.

Several hours later I left with my mind whirling deliriously. I felt ecstatic as if I had experienced a divine transformation. I staggered home drunk with revelation. My phone rang several times on the way.

The first couple of calls were the appointments I had missed that afternoon and I made some half-hearted apologies. I could tell they were not too impressed but I didn't care. Another couple were from new clients, referrals, I put them off. I tried to drink myself to sleep and spent the entire night dreaming of Lily. I would be making love with her and her face would change into the Chinaman's, making me wake parched and perspiring. The next morning I rose from my sweat soaked bed determined to resist my insane desire to once again visit Lily.

I would be strong. I was behaving like a prize idiot. All I had to do was occupy my mind with something else. Yes, that was it but what? I picked up a book but it was useless, I caved in after a pathetic couple of hours trying to read it. My mind would wander and all I could see was Lily's naked body. In the afternoon I went to her again. I know what you're thinking, you despise my weakness but I had to go! She was waiting for me and we made love again and again. When I left her I was in a state of near exultation. All I wanted to do was worship at the altar of Lilly.

The following days passed in a miasma of obsession. My mornings were spent in an agony of impatience. I thought briefly of going earlier but instinctively knew that there would be no one there to let me in.

My work suffered badly, very badly. I received a lot of calls from extremely annoyed clients threatening to take their business elsewhere if I didn't return calls, keep appointments and deal with their policies. I ignored them all and I completely lost track of time, I wasn't even aware what day it was. Every afternoon I was drawn towards that narrow passageway and the scented garden beyond. Every afternoon I would lose myself in hedonistic, sexual delights.

I lived for those few hours of extreme sensual pleasure in Lily's arms. The rest of life had no meaning for me.

The letters started to arrive. The first was from my landlords reminding me that the year's rental on my apartment was due. I chucked it in the bin. My head office sent me letters asking what the hell was going on saying they had received numerous complaints from clients. They went into the same place. My life started to disintegrate. I completely lost contact with everybody.

Then one day I went to the bank to draw some money and was shocked to find there was nothing left in my account. I'm not a good saver, never have been; which is a bit ridiculous really as I sell insurance. I live high, I spend a lot and had recently come back from a holiday in Japan that had wiped me out financially but I thought there was money still in there. I drew some out on my credit card and for the first time since this whole journey into depravity had started, I felt a twinge of panic. It's got to stop, I thought, It's got to bloody stop. I was still thinking this as I walked towards the opening metal gate.

Then about two weeks later after I'd pawned my flat screen TV and sold several other items in my flat, it did stop. Not through any strength on my part, it was because nobody came to open the gate. I waited for hours but nobody came. I waited until it got dark and then had to admit with a sinking feeling in my heart that nobody was going to come. I went the next day and the next and the day after that. I waited like a little puppy dog for a scrap of Lily to be thrown my way. I waited, not angrily but desperately. It was over, my life was over.

Without Lily my existence was pointless.

I started to wait by the passageway from early in the morning to late at night just in the hope that someone would come out or go in, someone that I could talk to about Lily, someone who would let me in to her. I became a curiosity in the street and the very beggars that I'd given money to in the past now laughed at me and called out 'Orang gala, orang gala' 'Crazy man, crazy man'. I didn't care. My eyes were riveted on the entrance to nirvana, hoping for a glimpse of my goddess.

I lost my flat, my job and all my possessions. My only clothes were the ones I had on and these soon became filthy and ragged. I slept by the gate. During the day I begged with my plastic cup.

'Meester, meester,' I cried and people would throw coins for me. I was no longer a curiosity I was just another piece of rubbish on the street. Then one day the gatekeeper came out of the passage and walked down the street. This was my chance, she could open the gate for me, and I shuffled after her. From another direction, I could see some child beggars also moving in on her.

A massive blow to my back knocked me to my knees. The few coins in my cup ran into the gutter. For a split second I was aware of a heavy boot swinging towards my face before it connected. It loosened some of my teeth and split my lips. I fell to the ground and curled up to try and protect myself. I caught a glimpse of my attacker as he kicked me repeatedly with his boots. I recognised him as one of the minders for the child beggars. I kicked out with my legs and caught him on the knee. He went down and then I was on him.

I took him by the throat and squeezed as hard as I could, banging his head on the ground. I pulled myself to my feet, dragging him with me. Using all my strength I heaved him into the air and threw him to the ground where he lay unmoving. Was he dead? I didn't care. I stood gasping for breath, pain all over my body.

'I was mistaken when I said I saw no violence in you Mr Spendlove,' said a voice behind me. I turned to see the Chinaman standing with Lily. I ignored him and looked at Lily. I saw nothing; no recognition, no sign of shared passions. She looked at me blankly and was there a hint of distaste in the curl of her lips? As if she were looking at a piece of street trash which is what I'd become.

In that instant, my longing for her withered and died and I saw a side to her that was ugly and unforgiving. I turned back to the China man; he still had that inscrutable smile on his face.

'Why?' I asked him, 'Why?'

He shrugged. 'What do you Westerners say?' he asked. 'No such thing as a free lunch?'

'Christ in heaven man!' I exclaimed. 'Is all this just a game to you?'

He smiled again.

'Watching you has been amusing,' he said, 'but now I'm bored. Goodbye Mr Spendlove.'

He turned to go and I could only stare at him in horror. What did he mean by 'watching me was amusing'? An awful thought crossed my mind - I remembered the large mirror on the wall. I moved to stop him.

'Wait a minute,' I said, reaching out to him.

A spitting hellcat that was Lily was suddenly in front of me and I found myself sitting on the ground. The China man turned back to look at me, a sneer on his face.

'Why do you Westerners always think that everything is yours by right?' he said. 'You always want your cake and eat it, yes? All life is just a game, Mr Spendlove, just a game. The question you should ask yourself - are you playing by your rules or someone else's?'

Then they turned and moved away. I watched Lily's body sway, a sight that only recently would have driven me crazy with lust but now it left me flat and empty. I watched them go until they were out of sight. I stood up and looked around and a few curious bystanders shrank away from me.

I straightened my body and walked away, leaving the perfumed garden behind forever.

McGREW'S SHOE

'Mad McGrew lives in a shoe. Just who, just who is Mad McGrew?'

The rhyme went through my head as I turned off the ignition to my car and looked at the shoe. Actually, to be exact it was a boot. An eighteen foot high, hollow replica of a stout walking boot that stood near the road leading to the small town where I used to live.

Attached to the heel and back portion of the boot was a large hoarding on which a faded blue arrow pointed. Underneath were the words 'Welcome to Tanglefoot: Population 23,472' and the once proud statement, 'Home of Weatherfast Footwear Inc.'

My father used to chant 'Mad McGrew lives in a shoe' whenever we drove past it. My two younger sisters would vie with each other to be the first to spot it and then shout 'I can see the shoe-oo, I can see the shoe-oo.'

I remember it came after a curve and dip in the road and then as we drove over the rise, there it was. I could tell that each of my sisters was hoping that the other had drifted off into a daydream and forgotten to keep a look out. Invariably they would call out simultaneously and then my father, with a smile on his face, would begin his chant.

I think I better explain. Tanglefoot was once a town that was going places. 'Weatherfast Footwear Inc.' employed a sizeable portion of the population. The money that was generated flowed in and out of various pockets and tills buying all the goods we think we cannot live without. We all benefited from Weatherfast's prosperity. It was a very popular footwear indeed and not just in Tanglefoot but all around the country. Highly reliable, 'made the old fashioned way', expensive but built to stay the course. 'Take a step up in life' was their slogan and people did. Orders flowed in. Oh yes, we had a lot to thank Weatherfast for.

So the town council and wise burghers of Tanglefoot raised no objection when Joseph Last, the owner of Weatherfast, suggested the larger than life hollow boot. It was regarded as a sculpture, a work of art. Tanglefoot was truly proud of its outsize boot. After all Tanglefoot was Weatherfast and Weatherfast was Joseph Last. Or to be strictly accurate Joseph Last and son for there was an heir to the Weatherfast legacy. A sole heir since Mrs Eloise Last had died in childbirth due to an unexpected haemorrhage which Tanglefoot's hospital staff had been completely unable to stem. The gift of life was literally paid for in blood and the whole ghastly incident ironically took place in the recently donated Joseph Last Maternity wing.

The Weatherfast streamlined efficiency went into a lull as Joseph Last slipped into a prolonged period of mourning. He was truly inconsolable with grief as he deeply loved his wife Eloise. He was a plain, unprepossessing man. Quiet, shy and extremely bashful where women were concerned and yet Eloise was somehow drawn to him. Much to everyone's surprise as she was considered to be a local beauty, full of laughter and gaiety and always had a hungry group of men with their tongues hanging out following her around.

Of course there was spiteful gossip and much talk about gold-diggers and dark predictions over covens of coffee mornings that Joseph Last would not last long and they wondered just how much he was insured for. In the main though, people shrugged their shoulders and said there was no accounting for taste. They wished them good luck and enjoyed the lavish reception that was thrown after the wedding. Indeed so sumptuous was the feast that it was the talk of the town and the surrounding areas for a great time afterwards.

Weatherfast as I said was Joseph Last. He held the reins completely and never let them go. So when he absolved control and slipped into his deep, brooding grief there was no one to take over and the factory floundered. Orders were missed and buyers started to look for alternative sources. Then all of a sudden he seemed to come to his senses took control once again and Weatherfast Footwear was striding forth once more, much to everyone's relief. The damage though was done and the granite confidence that the market had placed in Weatherfast had taken a knock. Cracks had appeared in its loyalty.

Joseph Last had changed too. Never an outgoing sort of person, he grew even more taciturn and withdrawn. It wouldn't be fair to the man to say he blamed his son for his wife's death but the child certainly grew up without his father's love. His father's wealth meant he never lacked for anything, anything that is except warmth and affection. His father avoided him as much as possible. Not because he actively disliked his son but he was a busy man and Conway also bore a striking resemblance to his mother. For Joseph Last the pain this evoked was too much to bear.

I think it was sometime around then, I must have been nine or ten years old, that McGrew appeared in the shoe. Tom Belling told me first. We were in school and he came running up to me full of excitement.

'Hey guess what?'

'What?' I asked, trying to get the bubble on my gum to cover my face without popping.

'My Pa was coming back from Oakleaf last night and he said he saw lights shining out from those small windows on the boot.'

'What boot?' I asked, not really being with it as my concentration was fixed solely on the biggest bubble I had ever blown in my life.

'The boot, dog breath, the boot on the Oakleaf road just out of town.'

Pop! The gum spread all over my face.

'Wow' I looked at him, my eyes wide.

'He said they kind of flickered but when he got close, they went out.'

This news spread like a forest fire. It soon developed into witches, spirits and gangs of bloodthirsty murderers waiting to jump out and cut the throats of unsuspecting motorists. We did not know how prophetic that last idea was to become. Soon after this the Sherriff and his deputy snuck up there to put an end once and for all to all the rumours. All they found was a blanket and a couple of candle stubs and they reckoned it was just kids fooling around or a couple, who had sneaked out of town for somewhere really private, if you know what I mean.

Anyway next day they put a big padlock on the door and that was the end of that. Or so we thought until someone saw the lights again. When the police went to check, they found the lock still in place. When that news got out, it really spooked us up. It was a big lock the Sherriff had put on, one with a hasp the size of a large finger and it was completely unmarked. Nobody had touched it.

Pop told us on account of he went bowling with Jim Rodgers the deputy. I'll never forget the night he told us. We were sitting around the table and had just finished a big plateful of Mom's fried chicken. It must have been Thursday because we always had chicken on Thursday nights. I can smell that chicken now. Anyway Pop said Jim Rodgers had told him that when they opened up the door, they found another blanket and some more candles even though they left the place empty after the first time.

'They found something else this time,' said Pop. Then he waited, drawing out the excitement. At last I couldn't stand it no more.

'What was it?' I asked, my voice coming out as a squeak. There was a loud sound of air being let out as my sisters stopped holding their breath.

'They found a large knife,' Pop whispered, sotto voce. 'With blood stains on it.'

'Wow,' said my sisters and I together.

'Was there a body Pa?' I asked. My sisters squealed.

'Hush John,' said Mom. 'You'll give them kids nightmares.'

'There was no body son,' Pop smiled. 'But they did find the words 'McGrews Shoe' carved into the wood on the floor.'

'Now that's just plain fancy,' said Mom.

'No Alice as I live and breathe, that's what Jim said they found. Those very words, now what do you make of that?'

'It's probably some bum who'll be moving on,' said Mom.

It seemed she was right for nobody saw anything suspicious for years. That didn't stop Pop from his silly chant every time we passed the boot and as time passed he added a couple of ghostly chuckles for effect.

Then I got a scholarship to go to college. Mom and Pop were so proud of me and Mom fussed and clucked around me, you know the sort of thing.

'John do you think we should get some more underwear, you know the thermal kind? It can get really cold up there.'

My sisters would giggle and tease but I knew they were real proud too. Pop kept on giving me 'advice', man to man sort of advice. We were too busy for a while to give even a passing thought to the strange McGrew and the Tanglefoot boot.

It was just as well I got the scholarship as times were hard. The whole country was slipping into a depression and people were finding it really difficult to make ends meet. Orders slipped away at Weatherfast and for the first time ever workers were laid off. Soon other shops started to close down in Tanglefoot and 'To Let' signs were going up in windows.

I'd been in college a couple of years when Mom wrote to me that lights had been seen again in the boot. I smiled when I read that and could hear my father chanting 'Mad McGrew who lived in a shoe'.

Her next letter though completely stunned me. It seemed a young teenage girl, only sixteen, had been brutally attacked, raped and then horror of horrors had her throat cut. The whole town was in shock. Nothing like that had ever happened in Tanglefoot before. Okay so it wasn't exactly a crime free Utopia. There had been robberies, violence, even the odd case of murder in its history but never this. This was shocking in its savagery and the youth of the girl involved.

The police found no clues, absolutely nothing that could help them solve the case. They stopped looking after a while and though the case stayed open, everyone knew they had given up. It changed the folks of Tanglefoot and left them with a nasty taste in their mouths. There were no more incidents. They held the inquest and the poor family of the girl buried the body and tried to get on with their shattered lives.

A few months later Pop died suddenly. Heart attack the doctor said. We couldn't understand it because he'd always been so fit.

Mom went to pieces. I got leave from my college and came home to be with her and my two sisters. God it was an awful time. I kinda had to stay in control of the funeral and all the shitty stuff that goes with someone dying. His going left this big hole in our lives and we sort of rattled around in it bumping into each other. Luckily Pop had quite a heavy life insurance, so Mom and the girls were taken care of and I still had my scholarship. Mom also had her job working in one the stores down town, so we were kind of well off, which is a sick way of looking at it really.

One morning Mom and I had been to the

lawyers to sort out a couple of things about Dad's will and life policy and were coming down the steps from the lawyer's office when I saw Conway Last. He was crossing the road towards us. Now he and I had never been what I would call close friends but for some reason he had taken a shine to me when we were at school together. I think it was because I didn't tease him like the others did and I tried to talk to him occasionally. Hell I knew the guy was kind of weird, jumpy and nervous and not much fun to be around but I did feel kind of sorry for him having no mom an all. The trouble is he started following me around like a puppy dog so I got to avoiding him.

My first instinct was to pretend I hadn't seen him and head in an opposite direction but before I could decide if I was going to do that, he smiled and waved at me so there was nothing for it but to wait for him to come across to us.

'Hi,' he said, 'I thought it was you,' then nothing. Just like the old Conway from school, he just stood there shuffling his feet.

'Hello Conway,' said my Mom.

'Hi Conway,' I said and just stood there waiting. I was feeling irritable and really didn't feel I had the patience or the energy to deal with him just then. I was hoping he'd go away when he suddenly surprised me.

Turning to my mom he said, 'I…uh…just

wanted to say I was real sorry to hear about your husband Mrs. Rivers.' Then he stuck out his hand to me. 'If there's anything you want or anything I can do, just ask.'

'Why thanks Conway,' I said, 'that's real nice of you.' He smiled nervously, nodded and walked away.

'I swear that boy gets to look more like his mother every day,' said Mom.

It shook me out of my thoughts.

'Huh, what's that you say Mom?'

'That boy, Conway, is just like his mother. The same hair, the same eyes and tall like she was too.'

'Cissy's got the same hair too,' I said. Cissy is one of my twin sisters. Although they are twins, they don't look alike at all. Cissy and Daisy are as different as, well as chalk and cheese. Daisy is the spunkier of the two, always getting into scrapes. She also always, always has an answer even if you haven't got a question. She takes after Pop with her fair sort of gingery hair. Cissy takes after Mom. She has the same large, dark eyes and the same hair, almost blue black in colour. Cissy is also the dreamer of the family always off in a world of her own making.

I dropped Mom back at the house and then went for a drive. I was still feeling edgy and angry. I was angry at God for taking my father and leaving us alone. I was angry at the stupid jerk in front of me who couldn't decide whether he was turning right or left. I leant on the horn and the poor guy got so flustered he stalled. Slamming the gears into second I pulled around him, cursing loudly. The old Chevy we drove farted and belched fumes like some incontinent Rhino. I made it worse by gunning the engine like some punk kid in his first hot rod. All of a sudden I just felt so pissed and waves of anger and sadness swept through me. I headed out of town away from the traffic and the people before I killed somebody.

Some guiding hand or automatic memory kicked in so without any recollection of driving, without any recollection of conscious decisions I found myself parked by McGrew's shoe. Then I couldn't hold back my pain and rage any longer and roared and wept smashing my hands against the steering wheel of the old Chevy. I can't remember how long I was there but it must have been a good couple of hours as the sun was beginning to dip. I calmed down a bit and sat there in a state of numb shock just blankly looking out of the windscreen.

'Do you wanna smoke, son?'

'Jesus!' I jumped so high in my seat I bumped my head on the roof of the car.

'Sorry son, didn't mean to startle you. Just thought you might need a smoke.'

I looked out of my window at the face to go with the voice. It was a kind looking face. A bit battered and wrinkled but the eyes had humour, warmth and concern in them. He stood a couple of feet from the car and was holding out a pack of Luckies. He was short, his clothes had seen better days and his hair was long and grey. I rubbed my head tenderly while looking at the proffered smokes.

'Huh, no I don't' but realising that sounded a bit ungracious added, 'but thanks mister.' He stood silently looking at me for a moment then tapped himself a butt out of the packet and lit it. He drew the smoke in with a great rush of air into his lungs and started coughing. When he finished, he took another deep drag, spat on the ground and smiled at me.

'I think you got the right idea son, perhaps I should quit. These things will kill me soon enough.'

Then he gave me a penetrating look. The silence seemed to stretch on elastic, expanding, filling time as it went. Then he nodded and said, 'Want to talk about it son?

I was a little surprised. I mean, hell, here was a total stranger. He could be a complete asshole for all I knew. I was about to tell him I was fine and was reaching for the ignition keys when something made me look at his face. His eyes just looked into me, compassion radiated from them and I found myself blurting it all out. The pain, the anger, the petulant isolation I had put myself into trying to keep it all together for my mom and sisters. He put a warm, comforting hand on my shoulder as I let it all out. He didn't say anything. When I'd finished or at least slowed down to the odd sigh and curse, he squeezed my shoulder.

'I don't know the answers son. I don't know why these things happen. They just do. It don't seem right somehow the good Lord taking a young man like your Pa for no reason or a small baby before it has a chance to grow. If we knew the answer then there'd be no reason for us being here. I do know this, if your Pa is watching over you right now, then he sure must be a proud man. He brought you up real fine son.'

He squeezed my shoulder once more and then turned and walked away. 'Anytime you want to talk son, you know where to find me.'

'Thanks mister,' I called after him and then he was gone.

As I drove home, I nearly crashed the car when I realised he must have been 'McGrew, McGrew who lived in a shoe'.

Another couple of weeks went by and I was just about ready to go back to college. Mom and the girls had settled down into the calming balm of routine. Then it happened again.

Another brutal, savage and totally mystifying murder. A pretty girl in her mid-teens like before. The whole of Tanglefoot went crazy. People started forming vigilante groups and patrolling the streets at night. The police tried to stop it but were helpless. As before they had nothing to go on, there were no clues and no murder weapon. Strangers in town were held, questioned and then released.

Joseph Last offered a ten thousand dollar reward for any information leading to the killer. He even formed his own vigilante group. Anyone in Tanglefoot who had a petty hate or grudge pointed a finger. The police wasted many hours checking spurious tip offs. It was a time of utter madness and even the withdrawn Joseph Last began behaving like a man possessed. He was out with his vigilantes every night and his lunacy seemed catching. People didn't seem to have any sense, just crazy talk and actions. The papers published photographs of the two murdered girls. I remember thinking at the time of how alike they were. The same big dark eyes set in pale, oval faces, the same long dark hair.

I had to go back to college but I couldn't leave Mom and the girls, not now, not with a killer on the loose. I decided to stay a few weeks more and phoned the college to explain. I could see Mom was glad I was staying a while longer.

I took the opportunity to go through some old papers and stuff of Pop's. I knew Mom couldn't tackle it as she was still hurting pretty deep. Whenever I came across an old photograph of Pop, I would sit and sob my heart out. I found an old newspaper cutting with a picture of Pop receiving a bowling trophy from Eloise Last. She sure was pretty. No wonder Joseph Last went nuts when she died.

'Real pretty,' I thought.

There was something about the photograph that triggered a memory somewhere but I just couldn't get hold of it. Ah well, it would come.

Later I went into the kitchen and Mom was making supper. The house seemed strangely silent. 'Where are Daisy and Cissy?' I asked. The evening was drawing in and I didn't like the idea of the girls being out after dark.

'They went to the movies' she said. 'They should be back soon.'

'I'll take the car there and give them a lift back,'' I said heading out the door.

'Ok,' said mom smiling at me, 'but they'll probably be waiting here when you get back.'

I got into the old Chevy, backed it out of the drive and drove it downtown. I saw Daisy standing at a stop, waiting for a bus. I couldn't see Cissy. A feeling of cold panic swept through me. I gunned the Chevy into a tight u-turn barely checking my speed and pulled up at the stop braking hard. I jumped out of the car.

'Daisy what the hell do you think you're doing? Where's Cissy, for Chrissake?' I realised I was shouting and other people at the stop had backed away. I took a couple of deep breaths and said as calmly as I could, 'Daisy this is real important, I'm not mad at you but you must tell me where Cissy is.' She started to cry.

'I told her you'd be mad. Mom said for us to stick together but Cissy said I was being silly. I don't know what she sees in that creep anyway.' At that my heart went cold.

'Get in the car,' I said. I put my foot down to the floor and kept it there until we got back. As I drove, Daisy told me how Cissy had been seeing this guy on and off for a few months. Not dating him as such, just meeting him for coffee, things like that.

'Who is he Daisy?' I asked.

'Conway Last,' she said.

Then it all fell into place. That picture of Eloise Last in the paper and who it reminded me of. The two girls who'd been murdered. The same big dark eyes, the same long, blue black hair framing the same pale faces. Just like Cissy. I tried to keep my voice calm but the words when they came out came through clenched teeth and had fear all over them.

'Where'd they go Daisy?'

'To his house,' said Daisy. 'To listen to records.

I tried to think calmly and rationally. Now Conway knew Cissy and Daisy were together. Good. Cissy would be safe because Daisy knew where she was going.

'Did Conway say anything else about where they might be going or what they were going to do, anything at all?'

'I don't know,' she said. 'I never spoke to him, Cissy wanted to meet him on her own.'

'So how do you know they were going to his place?'

'At the end of the film,' she said. 'Cissy told me in the toilet.'

'Oh God no,' was all I could say. I pulled into the drive of our house and honked the horn. Mom came running out.

'Get out,' I said to Daisy. The poor girl couldn't get out fast enough.

'Call the police,' I yelled to Mom. 'Cissy's at the Last place with Conway. He's the guy Mom. I think he's the guy.'

As I spun the car into the street, I caught a glimpse of Mom's face looking puzzled at first before a look of horror went across it. Then she was running for the phone.

I drove up the sweeping drive and bumped over the lawns to the back where I knew Conway had his room. Joseph Last would be out with his vigilante group so there would be no one there except Conway and Cissy. I stepped on the brakes and was out and running before the motor stopped.

Then I heard Cissy screaming. I didn't stop to think, I just ran at one of the windows and jumped right through the thing, wood glass and all. I landed in the room, rolled and came to my feet. Cissy was crouching there screaming and Conway was standing with a knife in his hand. I don't know who was more surprised Cissy or Conway. Then I just roared with fury as I leapt across the room to Conway. His hand came up with the knife but it was like it was in slow motion. I just knocked it out of the way and hit him hard on the jaw. I hit him with all the rage and fury in my body and his head snapped back and he poleaxed to the floor.

Then Cissy was in my arms sobbing. I stroked her and told her she was safe and everything was going to be ok. I could hear the police sirens and then a pounding on the door out front. I held on to Cissy and we made our way to it. Jim Rodgers was standing there.

Before he could say anything I said, 'He's in a room out the back. There's a knife on the floor. Probably the same knife he used before.'

His face set hard and then he was running, pulling out the cuffs as he went.

We went and stood by the police car. The police woman, who was there, got a blanket out of the car and put it around Cissy. The radio in the car crackled and then the Sheriff's voice came through as clear as a bell.

'Jim you there? I need your help. I got a vigilante problem at the Weatherfast boot. Seems they caught some hobo. Only hope I can get there before they do something stupid.' I didn't wait to hear any more.

'Look after Cissy,' I said.

Then I was sprinting round the back to the Chevy. It seemed only seconds before I was pulling out of the driveway and heading out of town to the boot. I knew I was too late when I saw the lights coming towards me and I recognised Joseph's Last's big, black Pontiac.

When I got there, McGrew was hanging with a rope around his neck. They'd fixed the rope to the top of the boot and hung him from it. Underneath him trampled into the ground was his pack of 'Luckies'. Too late to quit now I thought. I went round the back of the boot. The lock was snapped off.

The Sheriff's car pulled up as I walked into view. He got out and looked at me. His face seemed very tired and grey.

'Hello son,' he said. 'Jim just told me what happened.' He looked up and saw McGrew dangling on the end of the rope.

'Shit, what a mess. What a fucking mess. I think your Ma and sisters would like to see you. Are you okay to drive?'

'Yeh,' I said and got in the Chevy and drove home.

They left the boot there as a memorial to the whole shameful incident. Some of the folks were all for tearing it down but Joseph Last insisted it stayed. We moved away after the trial. Too many memories.

It turned out Conway blamed his mother and her death for his father's total lack of love and affection. Somewhere in his mind he started the killings as a way of punishing her. The factory went bust soon after and the town sort of folded in on itself.

I'm a lawyer now, doing well too. I got a new client who lives in Tanglefoot so that's why I'm parked here looking at McGrew's Shoe. I smoke now too, yeh that's right, 'Luckies'. I lit one for the old man and drew the smoke deep into my lungs just like he had done. Then I flipped the butt out of the window.

As I pulled away a movement caught my eye and I slammed on the brakes. In my rear view mirror I could see someone standing next to the boot. I knew him instantly. It was Joseph Last.

His face was carved with pain. Not as I remember him when they led him stumbling from the courtroom after they found Conway guilty. Then the pain was in its infancy. Now it had done time. So here he was living out his penance in old McGrew's shoe. Our eyes locked. Then I put the car into first and pulled away.

TO THE TOP

I always knew I would make it to the top. Always knew I would be numero uno, the king pin, be a success.

I have an undying faith in myself. Even at the lowest points in my life I never lost that faith. No matter how grim things got I always knew there would be another day when they would get better.

This was one of those days and here I was literally going to the very top of the vast block of blue and white concrete, stainless steel and huge windows that was the flagship building of the McDuck Corporation.

I was on my way to the executive suite which was a combination of offices, private apartment and landscaped terrace and of course a pool. It even included a putting green with bunkers to practice those devilishly difficult chip shots. This nestled amongst the water features shaded by the willows and maples and the handful of two hundred year old bonsais specially flown in from China by the man himself, William McDuck (pronounced Duke not quack quack). Not that I had ever seen it in person but 'The Businessman', the 'magazine no executive should be without', had run a profile on McDuck with emphasis on where he lived and worked. He was my mark, so I did my homework.

I figured that the guy liked plants. Not too hard to work that one out. Hell, only six months ago he had spent an obscene amount of money buying up vast tracts of rainforest in South America and chunks of forest and mountains in North America. He then set up trusts and commissions for the preservation of flora and fauna in these areas. I had seen him interviewed on television a few times and he came across as genuine, someone with no side to him; a straight forward, no bullshit, look you in the eyes and give you a firm hand shake, honest person. An anachronism in the corrupt, self- satisfying times we live in and I liked him. This made it all the more difficult to relieve the guy of some of his money but hey, I'm a professional, so it didn't worry me for too long.

The only bit of this deal that still bothered

me was the ease in contacting McDuck. It had been ridiculously simple. I had phoned his corporation, was put through to his PS and before I knew it I was speaking with McDuck himself. Now here I was hurtling up towards the biggest pay check of my career. But the bait had been too tasty for him to refuse. A straightforward guy he might be but you don't become the CEO of multi mega corporations and a billionaire without having an ego to match. I put his almost obsessive desire to 'save the world' together with his vanity, threw it into the water and bingo he bit! The idea was simple but with an edge. The best ones normally are.I just told him that while trekking through the Amazon, something I had done a few times as a very keen amateur horticulturist, specializing in South American plants, I came across a species I had never seen before. I checked and double-checked and was convinced it was a species of plant, which had never been recorded. I knew where to find it and would show him for a price. He could give it his name. I even had a photo of it! Courtesy of my computer, aren't they just dandy little machines.

Of course he asked me why I didn't have the honour of naming it myself. My answer was simple, I needed money. I figured two hundred grand was not an outlandish price to be asking, steep but not too steep. I would ask for half the money upfront and then I would do my runner. The amount I was asking for was enough to make all my effort worthwhile but not too much to receive a scoffing rejection. I wanted to hook my fish not chase it off. For somebody worth billions it was the equivalent of paying a few thousand for a personalized number plate and look at the kudos, look at the honour. Hell, with his track record and status it could lead to an award from the UN or whatever.

I smiled at the thought. Not because it was a ridiculous fantasy but because it wasn't. It could lead to further international honours and McDuck knew that. It was the possibilities that could stem from it all that would intrigue the man.

No, I was smiling at my imagination, it was unstoppable. My ma always said I would day dream my life away. I loved the creation of something tangible, solid and believable from just pure thought. I loved creating something so believable that even I believed in it, that was the beauty of it all. And it was beautiful, it was art. It was the creation of a symphony of bullshit that could vanish in a second and only I could hold it all together. I didn't need to embellish it with emotional schmaltz like a niece fighting cancer and hospital bills to pay which as it happens is true but I never like mixing work with family.

I love my brother Jim and his family. He's

everything I'm not. He's an honest, hardworking guy who works for a bakery. Been with them twelve years and will probably be with them until the day he dies. His wife Shirley is a doll and makes the best meatloaf and gravy I ever tasted and wow is she a looker! Did a bit of modelling, you know catalogue sort of stuff, before she fell for Jim. Their kids have the sweetest, most natural personalities I've come across. They are a tribute to their parents. The boy Jack is eleven years old, tall for his age and has a smile that brightens the darkest day. Nerice is nine, has her mother's beauty and man I'm just putty in her hands. She's the one who is in and out of hospital at the moment fighting the big C and being a very, very brave girl.

You know, I'm an easy going sort of guy; I try not to get steamed up about stuff. In my line of work, it pays to stay cool, to be one step ahead of those around you. But it sure makes me mad when I think of Nerice and then see some of the creeps and jerks walking this planet.

Jim has got insurance but not enough. I know he needs money, he hasn't told me how much but I know it's a chunk.

Now it just so happens that I'd been wracking my brains to think of a scam big enough to get the kind of money Jim needs. This was made all the more difficult because I had to keep a low profile due to some very angry bookies that were looking for me. I was staying in a small apartment I use sometimes when things get hot. Nobody knows about this place, not even Jim and Shirley. I just tell them I have to go out of town on business and will be back soon. Then I get some beers, some bacon, some smokes and watch old movies until people get tired of looking for me.

I was flipping channels when I caught an interview with McDuck; something about his face stopped me pressing the button. It was an honest face and he spoke sincerely. He also looked roughly my age, in his early forties. McDuck was a man who had sprung into prominence in the dot com boom, got out at the right time, made millions and his star had not stopped ascending since. I listened for a while as he talked about his passion for preservation and as he talked an idea grew in my head.

That was the easy bit. I am very sincere and convincing when I want something and this story was plausible and just farfetched enough to sound genuine. The hard work was the background. Like I said I do my homework. For several weeks I trolled through the Internet and went to the central library. I studied and learnt facts about every South American plant I came across. Did you know there's a plant called the Nepenthes or 'Monkey Cup' that can catch and eat small birds, mice and frogs? Man that freaked me out when I read about that. Reminded me of a movie I saw once, about plants that ate people, 'Day of the Triffids' I think it was called. I thought it was a bit of science fiction nonsense at the time, not so sure now.

One day in the central library I looked up from what I was reading and saw 'Big Bernie' taking some books out at the counter. I slid down in my seat and propped the book I was reading in front of my face. Luckily it was a large book of illustrations so he didn't see me. I was down to Bernie for about four grand and I've known people disappear for less. What surprised me was that Bernie could read! Aw come off it, that's too ridiculous an assumption. Maybe he was getting some books for his mother, yes that had to be it. A good boy to his ma is our Bernie. It was that which made me realize I'd done enough research. I had to get moving on this one. I needed the money fast. Needed to help Jim out and needed to get gorillas like 'Big Bernie' off my back.

So I looked in yellow pages until I found a college of horticulture and then phoned them up. I explained about my interest in South American plants and asked if they knew of any clubs or societies that specialized in those plants. You wouldn't believe how many there are. I tell you man it's a growth industry. Anyway I chose a couple of likely looking ones and phoned them up to get times and dates of meetings. I was in luck, there was one meeting that night in the Hall of the Ancient Buffalo, [I kid you not!] So I 'shuffled off to Buffalo'. Now some of you old music freaks will get that allusion. Not my kind of music, I only know it because I actually come from the place originally. My ma got kind of nostalgic for the place before she shuffled off herself and used to play the record all the time.

That was in the days when they still had black discs of plastic that you reverently placed a needle upon and the voice of the juju man would issue forth. I think I've still got a disc of 'Shuffle off to Buffalo' somewhere but of course nothing to play it on.

I passed with flying colours. Drank coffee and cheap wine and talked all night with other members about my recent trip to Brazil. I surprised even myself with my knowledge. I knew I'd cracked it when someone suggested I should give a talk about my field trips. The only dodgy moment was being asked the name of the hotel I stayed in when I got to Brazil. Now that's the sort of detail I pride myself on knowing but cutting corners because of seeing Bernie had left holes in my research. I just said I couldn't remember off hand but could get it to them if they needed it. All in all it was a very successful evening and I now felt ready to contact McDuck.

The elevator came to a halt, the doors opened soundlessly, I stepped forward and there I was in the sanctum of sanctums. A gorgeous brunette, heels clicking on the marble floor came towards me hand outstretched. 'Mr Beaver?' I flashed my best smile.

'Yes, that's right, Miss..?'

'Swan,' she replied. 'Ms Swan,' she politically corrected me. 'I spoke to you on the telephone. I'm Mr McDuck's private secretary.'

'Oh yes of course,' I said. 'I don't know why but I expected someone ...'

'Older?' she finished for me.

I smiled wryly at her, 'I'm sorry Ms Swan, I didn't intend to patronise.'

She smiled back. 'Think nothing of it, Mr Beaver, no offence taken. By the way, curious name Beaver, not many in the phone book.'

'Yes we're an endangered species,' I said laughing. All the while thinking she's been checking up on me, careful of this one, she's sharp. 'I'm not in the phone book. The contact number I gave you is my mobile phone.'

'Yes I know. From out of town?' she asked. 'Where are you staying?'

My brain went into scramble.

'I'm renting a small apartment, south side,'

I replied. Now the trick to fabrication is to keep it as simple as possible and to tell as much truth as possible. The more truth you can insert in your story the more believable it becomes. But there was something about her questions that made me feel like I was on the witness stand. I kept my smile in place.

A door opened and a big man stepped into the foyer. I recognised him immediately, William McDuck.

'Bill,' she said. 'This is Mr Beaver.'

'Thank you Jenny, I'll take it from here. Oh and chase up that contract from Gibbons, his lawyers have had it long enough to check it a dozen times. Look through the alterations if any and let's see if we can tie it up by the weekend.'

'I'll get on to it right away,' she said and disappeared into another office.

Bill and Jennie I thought to myself now that sounds very familiar. I wonder if there's anything going on between the two of them. I know he's not married but she might be. Information like that could be useful in how to play a situation. I thought I'd try a little gentle probing.

'Ms Swan is a very attractive woman,' I ventured. I thought I'd gone too far as he gave me a questioning look and there was a very long pause before he answered me.

'Yes, isn't she?' he said. 'Top of her year at Harvard Law College. Why she chose to come and work for me I still don't know.'

Ah, so that's why it felt like being questioned by the DA.

'Well Mr Beaver, you better come into my office. We have a lot to talk about,' he said turning and walking away. I dutifully followed, mentally focussing myself for the game to come.

The first thing that struck me when I walked into McDuck's office was the light streaming through the sliding glass doors that connected the office with the landscaped roof terrace. There were a few pieces of wooden sculptures dotted around the room; they looked kind of African to me. The desk was also wood, big, solid and traditional. It was also bare of any paper work. There were a couple of telephones, an intercom and an open laptop. The desk was positioned so that with a slight turn of the large, high backed, leather chair behind it, you could see out onto the terrace. He walked over and sat down in that chair.

'Please sit down, Mr Beaver,' he said indicating one of two similar, though smaller chairs in front of the desk. I sat.

'Your telephone call intrigued me Mr Beaver. It wasn't a begging call and believe me I get many of them, I try to help out when I can, when I think it's a genuine case. It wasn't a threat or an attempted blackmail and I've also had a few of those in my time. No, it was a straightforward business deal. I like things like that. You say you have found a hitherto unknown plant in Peru and will show me the location of this plant for two hundred thousand dollars and I can say I discovered it.'

'Yes, that's about it, except it wasn't Peru it was Brazil,' I said. If that's the best he can come up with, this is going to be easier than taking the proverbial candy from a baby, I thought.

'What makes you think I would be interested in this proposition?' he asked.

'I'm here talking to you now, aren't I?' I replied.

'Touché,' he replied and smiled. It was time for just a little bit of hard ball. In a con, never be the wanting party, always let your mark be the one who wants. Remember you are doing them a favour.

'Mr McDuck,' I said, 'before we go any further, I want you to know that there is a condition to this deal.' McDuck chuckled. I must admit that wasn't the reaction I expected; outrage, indignation, disbelief, rejection, any of these but not amusement.

McDuck sat quietly opposite me and continued to smile. I smiled back, this was fun! Eventually he spoke and I breathed an inward sigh of relief. In the game of negotiation, when somebody speaks, is as important as what they say.

'Every deal has conditions Mr Beaver,' he said. 'What are yours?'

This was it; this was the moment of truth. I kept my face neutral and impassive.

'I expect payment of half the money before we go to Brazil,' I said. McDuck continued to smile.

'Why should I trust you?' he asked. 'I could give you the money and you could walk away from here and disappear.'

'By the same token,' I replied, 'I could show you where the plant is and then you could deny all knowledge of me and refuse to pay.'

'True,' he said, 'it seems we have an impasse.'

'No impasse,' I said rising from my seat. We just have no deal. I know there are others who would be interested.'

'Sit down Mr Beaver,' McDuck said, still smiling pleasantly. 'I didn't say I wouldn't give you the money but I do need to hear what you have to say first, wouldn't you agree?' I nodded and sat down.

There was a tap on the door and the beautiful Ms Swan came in carrying a tray with a pot of coffee, cream, sugar and biscuits. She placed them on a small side table and turned to me. 'Is coffee ok?' she asked.

I smiled at her, 'Just fine.'

'Thank you Jenny,' said McDuck. 'Just leave it and we'll help ourselves.' I watched as she moved across the room to the door and boy did she move. She turned at the door and grinned at me. I grinned back. Steady boy, this is neither the time or place. Remember you're working.

After she'd gone, McDuck busied himself with the coffee. He looked at me and said, 'Black with two sugars?'

'Yes. How did you know?'

He grinned at me. 'I didn't, I just guessed.'

To my surprise he brought the coffee over to me and went and sat down again. He turned his chair to look out onto his garden.

I did the same and we sat in silence while we drank our coffee. I looked around for an ashtray but couldn't see any. I was dying for a smoke. One of the phones on his desk rang and broke the silence.

He swivelled round and picked it up. 'Yes Jenny? Oh good, thank you, I was wondering what you thought. Really? That is interesting, thank you. Make sure we're not disturbed will you.' He put the phone down.

'I did some checking on you Beaver,' he said.

I shrugged unenthusiastically, 'I would have been surprised if you hadn't but I have nothing to hide,' I said as blandly as possible. I sounded relaxed but my antennae were attuned to every nuance of every word being spoken. What worried me now was the lack of Mr when he had just used my name and I thought, uh oh something's coming that I'm not going to like.

'That's just the point Beaver, you have nothing to hide. I couldn't find any information about you; in fact you don't seem to exist.'

I tried to laugh it off. 'Well as I told Ms Swan earlier, not many of us Beavers left, we're an endangered species.'

'Then that should make it easier to trace you,' said McDuck, 'not more difficult. But there's nothing, not a whiff. You're not an endangered species Beaver, you're an extinct one.'

I laughed. 'That's very funny sir, very funny indeed. It's easily explained, I'm from out of town you see.'

'Oh yes, you did say on the phone, Buffalo wasn't it?' cut in McDuck.

So far so good, if he checked, he would find a guy called Beaver, about my age, who did come from Buffalo. The real Beaver had no family, both his parents died in a car accident when he was young, he then spent some years in a local orphanage and left Buffalo in his late teens to find his way in the world and promptly disappeared without trace. As I said, I do my homework. Beaver was an alias I had used a couple of times before.

'Yes Buffalo, that's right sir. Ain't been back in a while but I still think of the place fondly. I had a happy childhood there.' I said this sincerely - I meant it - I had a great time as a kid there.

'Yes, I do know the place,' said McDuck.

'You do?' I sounded surprised and I was surprised. Most people didn't know it existed.

'I passed through it once, a long time ago.'

I might have been mistaken but did I detect a hint of sadness in his voice? Maybe talking about my childhood brought back a memory of his, I don't know. I filed it away in case I needed it later.

Suddenly the mood changed as McDuck smiled broadly, relaxed back in his chair and said, 'Tell me about your last trip to Brazil and how you discovered your new plant. It must have been very exciting.'

'Oh it was,' I replied. 'But not my plant I reminded him, your plant.'

He laughed and said, 'Maybe, Beaver,

maybe. Now tell me.'

I allowed myself to relax too, as I was now on familiar territory. I launched into the story I had created. All my homework paid off as I dropped names of plants and trees all over the place, also adding little bits of local interest as I went along. I even added a couple of amusing incidents about people I had met along the way. I try not to get big headed because then mistakes can be made but boy I'm good. So good I even impress myself sometimes.

He listened carefully to everything I said, sometimes asking questions about plants and Brazil. Eventually I finished and he sat looking at me quietly, not speaking. Quite suddenly he began to clap, 'Bravo!' he said, 'That was brilliant.'

Again that was not quite the reaction I expected. I really couldn't buttonhole this guy. Then abruptly he reached inside his jacket pocket, pulled out his cheque book and started to write. 'A hundred thousand wasn't it?'

'Yes, that's right.' I managed to get the words out without squeaking which was amazing since my heart was going ten to the dozen and a voice in my head was screaming 'I've done it!'

He continued to speak as he filled in the cheque. 'You know Mr Beaver; I like to pride myself on being a good judge of character. There that's that.'

He signed his name with a flourish and handed the cheque over.

'Thank you,' I said as I took it. I glanced down at it and the cold feeling of reality began to creep down my spine. 'But this cheque is made out to Pointer,' I said.

'That is your name, isn't it?' he said softly, not taking his eyes from my face. I didn't reply for what seemed to be an eternity. Could I bluff this one? The answer was no.

'How long have you known?' I asked him, my voice flat and lifeless.

'Since the beginning,' said McDuck.

'So why didn't you call the cops?' I asked, feeling like someone had just dropped me from the top of the skyscraper I was sitting in.

'I don't know,' mused McDuck. 'I kind of got interested in your story. Besides which it was a good con. I liked your style.'

For once in my life, I was absolutely lost for words. I looked at the cheque in my hands, at the words one hundred thousand dollars, at the signature, William McDuck, now utterly worthless. He smiled at me.

'How does it feel to be conned,' he asked? I shrugged. What could I say? I put the cheque down on his desk.

'No keep it,' he said.

'Why? To frame it?' I asked, a slight bitterness I must admit, creeping into my voice.

'Present it,' he said, 'I'll honour it.'

I was astonished.

'But why,' He stood up, drawing an end to the whole hideous nightmare. I stood too; I just wanted to get away from there as quickly as possible. 'As I said, I liked your style. Besides you really do need the money or rather your brother does.'

This just blew me away, how much more did this man know about me. My hands shook as I picked up the cheque. He moved around his desk and ushered me out into the hall to the elevator.

'By the way,' he said, 'If you want a job working for me come and see me on Monday - I need a good bullshitter. You know what they say; it takes one to catch one. You will be my bullshit barometer.' He laughed at his joke. 'Are you for real?' I asked a bit testily. Ok, so I'm a con man but I am a professional and I was getting just a little bit fed up with being called a bullshitter.

'Very much so, Mr Pointer, very much so.' He stopped and looked me directly in the eyes. The straightforward look that I'd first admired about the man when I saw him on the television. His voice got serious.

'This is on the level. I've got a gut feeling about you, I'll think we'll get along just fine. By the way, Jennie thinks so too. A 'charming rogue' I think she called you,

"… but with an honest smile." I trust her instinct.'

Now that astonished me as I thought I'd got off completely on the wrong foot with that little lady.

'She does?' I frowned. 'But when could she have told… oh, of course the phone call.'

The elevator arrived and in an unreal state I stepped into it. I turned and faced him.

'When did you know?' I asked.

'From your first call.'

'But how?'

'Oh that's easy,' he said, 'Because I'm Mr Beaver from Buffalo.' The doors shut on his smiling face.

PAPATONG

The frantic whirring of trapped wings caught the attention of William Grothe. He had been idly dreaming about his native Holland, wishing he was back there and bemoaning the fact that he was stuck in this god-forsaken place in western Java. He looked up at the dragonfly as it vainly tried to exit the building by flying through the wall.

The heat was intolerable. Sweat trickled down his neck to an already saturated under vest which clung damply and uncomfortably to his body.

The dragonfly continued to uselessly throw itself against the badly plastered brick wall even though there was an open door not three feet from where it was.

'You and me, my friend. We're both where

we don't want to be and the way out is obvious'.

The dragonfly suddenly skittered down the wall and found the open door. It hovered for a split second, uncertain, then swooped and soared with the joy of freedom and was gone.

William sighed in recognition of the escape, not without a certain amount of envy.

'Ah well, back to bloody work', he mumbled to himself and hauled himself to his feet.

He was a tall man, with big, well-muscled bones, in his early 40s. Not good looking but then not bad looking either. He had a battered, rugged sort of face. His best feature were his eyes. They were bright, sky blue and looked out on the world with the direct gaze of an honest man. He had a broad smile which he used more and more infrequently these days. Not that he was unhappy in his work. In fact the waterway that he was building was going well and he derived enormous satisfaction and sense of worth from the creation of the canal. It was just… well it was just that he felt so alone. It wasn't just being on his own that bothered him; it had never been a problem before and to be honest it didn't really bother him now. Solitude and the chance to be with oneself was a welcome opportunity, a chance to reflect, a chance to plan. No, what he felt was a sense of complete isolation. Somehow even among all the people of the village where he lived he felt dislocated and lonely. This feeling was alleviated when he took an occasional trip to the nearest city and met other westerners. But with a deadline to meet these trips became more infrequent. Of course he could rationalize this feeling. He was a foreigner in a strange land and the Dutch were not particularly liked by the locals.

This didn't help his loneliness though. He wasn't exactly shunned but there was a coolness of attitude towards him. He felt that if he dropped dead nobody would care in the slightest; they would probably just step over his body and carry on with their lives. People were polite and carried out instructions but no one engaged with him.

Mr Hartanto was the local bigwig and landowner that he was dealing with regarding the area to be used in the building of the water way. He was a prime example of the polite hostility that he felt all the time. Hartanto was the epitome of good manners towards him but they didn't mean anything. William was sure they were a cover, a front for the reality of what was really felt in the soul of the man.

Here he was on his way to meet with Hartanto once more for another round of seemingly endless discussions over what land he could use. What made the whole palaver even more infuriating was the fact that what he was doing would actually improve Hartanto's land and therefore the value of it. Why couldn't the man see that? William already knew the answer to that question. He was persona non grata in Indonesia. He was hated because he was Dutch and the local people would do anything to make life difficult for him.

At first, he had thought their inability to carry out a simple order was due to a lack of education. On some days it did seem that his workers were unable to carry out his instructions with any degree of competence. It didn't take him long to realise there was a national conspiracy to be as obstructive as possible under the guise of miscommunication.

'Selamat siang tuan' said the woman sitting by the side of the path, that wound down from his house into the local kampong. Her raffia basket next to her, was full of bottles of 'jamu jamu' (a local selection of medicines and herbal drinks) that she was selling. He'd tasted some once. It was vile, an awful solution whose main ingredients seemed to be ginger and bitter turmeric. The local people swallowed it down as medicine, as a pick me up tonic, as a body shuddering blast to get the day started. She was a regular sight early in the mornings as his workers clustered round to get their shot.

'Siang,' he replied with a nod.

William enjoyed this walk through the

kampong, passing clove trees, cinnamon trees, coconuts, mangos, avocados and bananas in profusion. To his left he could see a range of mountains in the distance, many of them still actively volcanic. A grey mist was enveloping them, maybe a storm was brewing … he sighed and let his gaze sweep over the startling green of the rice fields. He loved that view best on this walk. It was such a calming, refreshing colour and never failed to uplift him. The air was clean and he breathed deeply enjoying the myriad scents of the spices and fruits.

Before long he arrived at the gates of Hartanto's house. A servant saw him coming and opened the gates for him. After closing the gates, the servant ran ahead to warn of his arrival.

It always struck William how beautiful the garden was, full of the most wonderful profusion of flowers, trees and shrubs, dazzling in their shades and colour. There was Frangipani, Jasmine, Angels' trumpets and one whole wall to his left covered in the most magnificent Morning Glory. The humming of the big black bees as they sipped the nectar of the blue flowers, accompanied him as he walked up to the front door.

The garden was all in complete contrast to his perception of Hartanto. These were the grounds of an expressive and sensitive being, certainly not the tight arsed, obstructive little bastard that Hartanto was. William shrugged off the thought.

Perhaps the garden was the wife's influence, although he doubted it. He had met Hartanto's wife a couple of times and she hadn't impressed him with the lush sensuality that pervaded the garden.

Even so, who knew what passion lies beneath the correct and staid exteriors of some of these reserved women? He smiled to himself - still waters can run very deep. The mental image of Mrs Hartanto in the throes of passion took him by surprise and made him laugh out loud.

'Good morning,' a voice said. 'You are happy?'

Startled, William's face flushed and he looked around but couldn't see anybody. He was surprised because the person had used English.

A young woman rose up from the ground where she'd been tending to some flowers and smiled at him. 'We have not met. My name is Putri. You have come to see my father yes?'

He noticed her English was slightly formal and stilted but then again so was his.

'Yes, that's correct,' he replied. 'You surprised me, I didn't see you. My name is Grothe.' He held out his hand. 'William.' he added a bit lamely.

She smiled at him. Her hand felt cool and soft. Her eyes looked humorously up at his and reluctantly he let it go, feeling flustered.

'Yes, I know your name.'

'Oh really, how do you ..? Oh, of course your father,' he trailed off weakly.

She nodded.

'You like working in the garden?' He was trying to think of something to say.

'Yes, when I can,' Putri replied. 'I like growing plants.'

'It's beautiful,' he said looking around him.

'Thank you sir.' Delightedly she clapped her hands together.

There was something about the radiance of her smile, her innocence, her energy that captivated him.

'Putri! Putri where are you?' An irate voice called in Indonesian.

'I'm here father, in the garden,' replied Putri also in Indonesian.

Hartanto came from the house. He looked shocked when he saw his daughter standing with William.

'What are you doing here? Get in the house at once.'

'Yes father,' she said, walking to the front door.

William was quite pleased to note that he understood most of what was spoken. He also noticed that Putri didn't seem at all perturbed by her father's temper.

She turned at the door and looked back at William. 'I hope we meet again,' she said in English, then went inside.

'Why are you here Mr Grothe?' Mr Hartanto asked rudely.

His voice snapped William back to reality away from the moment of magic that the young woman had created around him. He shook his head as if waking from a dream.

'You know why I'm here,' he returned just as rudely. 'I want a decision about the land and if I don't get one I might have to take matters further.'

Hartanto's attitude softened slightly. 'Yes, yes of course. Please come inside we will talk.'

William nodded and followed the Indonesian.

It was dark in the house, the narrow windows not letting in much light. He paused for a moment just inside the door to let his eyes adjust.

'This way Mr Grothe,' beckoned Hartanto almost anxiously, pointing to a small office off the hallway. They had used it for discussions before and it was the only part of the house, besides the hall, that William had been into. It was another brick in the wall of non-acceptance that he felt. One blessed relief was the cool shade, now that he was out of the sun.

'Sit, please.'

William sat.

One of the servants came in carrying a tray with coffee, water and biscuits and placed it on the desk. Bowing low she scuttled out of the room.

The two men took some coffee and sat silently looking at each other.

'It is very hot today.' Hartanto started the conversation.

'Yes,' William replied.

There was another long pause then Hartanto said, 'The rains will be here soon and then it will be wet.'

William sighed. This was a game they played each time they met. This pussy footing back and forth and exchanging of formalities until the true purpose of the meeting could be reached. He always found this customary social dance extremely frustrating and today he was not prepared to play it.

'Mr Hartanto,' he cut in abruptly. 'The waterway is about to cross some of your land and I need your permission in writing to continue building it. This I want today before I leave your house. You've had long enough to do this and I'm not prepared to wait any longer. I might add that I am asking you out of politeness. I do not need to do this and could take the land with force using the military. I do not wish to do this but I will do it if it is necessary.'

Hartanto exploded. Rising rapidly out of his chair he moved violently round the desk towards William. With great effort he stopped himself, gripping the edge of the desk until his knuckles were white, his face suffused with anger.

'Get out! Get out of my house!'

'Very well,' said William calmly, standing and walking towards the door. 'The military it is.'

He walked out of the house and down the path to the gates. Curiously enough he wasn't angry. In fact he felt quite pleased with himself. At last the situation between him and Hartanto was totally clear and he felt that they both knew where they stood. He had tried being reasonable with the man but it had got him nowhere. Now the gloves were off. He reached the gates and took a long look around the beautiful garden thinking of those soft, cool hands that had created it. He opened the gates and started along the road back the way he had come. Already he was planning what to do. First back to his house and then contact the Commander of the nearest garrison. A few troops stationed in the village would soon shake the locals up a bit.

He became aware of someone hurrying behind him and stopped to look. He recognised one of the servants from Hartanto's house. She came up to him breathing heavily having run the entire way and handed him an envelope. Then just as quickly she ran away. William opened the envelope and smiled. Inside was the agreement about the land signed and stamped by Hartanto. It was brief, terse and to the point, the frustration and anger practically writhing up from the words but it was enough.

Later that afternoon, as the sun was dipping, before the muezzin call to evening prayers, William was heading back to his house from the waterway. He was feeling very pleased with the work done that day. His men worked hard, digging and carrying. The waterway had taken a leap forward, more than double what was normally cleared in a day. If it carried on at that rate, he would be finished ahead of schedule.

To his surprise, he found Putri, Hartanto's daughter, waiting for him on his patio.

'Mr Grothe can I speaking with you,' she said.

Before he could stop himself he corrected her, 'Speak with.'

She blushed. 'Speak with, yes.'

Remembering their earlier meeting he asked, 'Does your father know you're here?'

She suddenly looked very flustered and uncomfortable –

'Because if he doesn't know I don't think you should be here.'

For a moment she seemed about to burst into tears and this horrified him.

'Look I don't know why you're here but you are welcome to rest awhile and have some tea with me,' he said. 'I was just going to make some.'

'Thank you, you are very kind.' She smiled.

He opened his door and ushered her into his lounge, indicating a chair where she could sit.

'Wait here, I won't be long.' By way of explanation he added, 'My maid only comes in the morning. I am a private man and like to tend to myself.'

When he returned with the tea, he found her reading a copy of Shakespeare's 'Hamlet' that he had left on the coffee table.

Embarrassed she quickly closed the book and put it down on the table.

'I'm sorry. Saya tidak sopan,' she said, reverting to Indonesian in her confusion.

William looked puzzled for a second, 'I am not polite' what did she mean? Then he realised she was apologising for reading his book.

'There is nothing wrong in reading my book,' he said. 'In fact you are welcome to borrow it if you want. I have just finished reading it. I think you will find the English very difficult, I did. Where did you learn to speak English?'

'In my school in Jakarta and from books,' she replied. 'I practice when I can.' She indicated the book with a delicate move of her hand and once again William found himself being fascinated by her grace and her poise.

'What is the story?'

'That's a good question and a difficult one for there are many stories in the story.' William smiled. 'Hamlet, the name of the play is the name of a young prince who has many difficult decisions to make. But he doesn't make any of them. Everything goes wrong for him and there is a tragic ending.'

She looked at him clearly confused and not understanding. Oh dear, he thought. This is getting complicated.

William also found it difficult to think clearly and logically. Something about the young woman confused him; she had such an entrancing way of looking at him with her head slightly to one side, her face open and full of enquiry.

'As I said before, it is difficult to understand, but please borrow it if you want. I have other books here if you want to look.'

Her face lit up and again, like at their first meeting in the garden, she clapped her hands together in delight. William felt his head beginning to spin and had to wrench his thoughts back to the reason for her being there.

'I'm sorry but I must ask you again, why are you here?'

This time there was no onset of tears, thank God. But what was even more off-putting was the way in which she gathered herself together to reply. William found something quite forceful, even formidable about it. This was clearly not a woman to be trifled with and he understood now her lack of reaction to her father's temper in the garden. It had simply not bothered her.

As if reading his thoughts she said, 'It is about my father I have come. He does not …, we do not want the military to come to our Kampong. It would be very bad and making the people very angry.'

William just managed to stop himself from correcting her English. 'Has your father sent you here?'

She looked shocked at the thought. 'No, he would be very angry with me if he knew I was here.'

William nodded. 'Well you need not worry, I will not tell him. Also do not worry about the military. With the paper that I now have from your father, they are not needed anymore.'

'Thank you Mr Grothe, thank you I am very happy now.' She rose from her seat. 'I must go, my father might ask for me.'

'Wait,' he said, desperately trying to think of something to make her stay. 'A book! Maybe you would like to borrow a book.'

She smiled up at him, 'Perhaps another time, Mr Grothe.'

'Of course,' he said. 'Please come round anytime and, um, call me William. Mr Grothe is a bit formal.'

'Thank you William.' She smiled again and William felt ridiculously happy.

When they stood outside his house, they could hear the muezzin calling the people to prayer. A little boy was waving his hands in the air and making a dragonfly dance before him.

'I have never seen that before. It looks like

magic, how does he do it?' William asked.

'Yes, it is like magic is it not?' She laughed. 'It's just a piece of cotton tied around a Papatong.'

'What's that?'

'You call it a dragonfly, I think.'

He smiled. 'Papatong, what a lovely name.'

The next few days were a nightmare of frustration for William. Every day when he returned to his house he hoped to find Putri waiting for him and every day he was disappointed. He had even selected a few books that he thought she might find interesting. He desperately wanted to see her and hear her voice again. To see the comical way she tilted her head to one side when asking a question, her eyes opening wide in querulous astonishment. His nights were full of dreams of her and every morning he would wake wrecked. In short, he was falling in love with her. He wanted to go to her house and ask to see her but he knew that would be a big mistake. So William waited and weeks passed with still no visit from Putri. As the time went by, the longing grew less and hardened into a cynical bitterness.

After discreet offhand enquiries with his maid, he discovered that Putri had gone to stay with relations in East Java several hundred kilometres away. William was surprised that she had left without saying goodbye but on further thought put it down to her age and rather surprising immaturity since she had not struck him as being a silly, empty headed girl. Ruefully he kicked himself for even thinking the way he had about her, called himself a silly fool, and threw himself into his work.

Now uppermost in his mind was finishing his contract and getting the hell out of Indonesia. It had begun to pall and though there were amusing interludes and occasional moments of the wonder and joy that he had originally experienced on coming to this country, his life now felt somehow empty, boring, and repetitious. He found he was growing more cynical about Indonesia every day. It was increasingly easier to find things wrong with the place and not look for what was good.

William drove his workforce hard and although there were many complaints he ignored them and pushed hard for completion. Then one morning as he was preparing to go to work and making idle conversation with his maid, she asked him if he knew that Hartanto's wife was very ill. He was surprised as not a scrap of this news had come to him via his workers or managers or even Hartanto himself, with whom he had had a rather frosty onsite meeting the day before about the time to be spent on his land.

When questioned, his maid revealed that Hartanto's wife was suffering from a virulent form of dengue fever. It was a mosquito-borne virus that attacked the blood and affected the brain. Nothing much could be done for it except cooling the patient as much as possible. One just had to let it run its course. There were different strains of fever some more virulent than others. It either killed or it didn't. For all his antipathy with Hartanto, William felt deeply sorry for the man. From what his maid had told him, it sounded as though Hartanto's wife had an extremely high fever and the situation was very dangerous. He decided to go and see Hartanto briefly to offer his sympathy and made arrangements with his maid to go and tell his managers that he would be late. He smiled wryly to himself as he knew that as soon as his workers received the news they would all squat down on their haunches and smoke their cigarettes.

When he arrived at Hartanto's house, William rang the bell hanging by the gates. It was a misty, grey morning, the sun not yet burning its way through. He thought the garden seemed sad and depressed.

One of the servants appeared and as soon as she saw who was standing outside the gates, quickly turned and ran back inside the house. Shortly after, Hartanto appeared and made his way to the gates. Something about the man shocked William. Hartanto seemed a mere shadow of his former bombastic self. He shuffled along the path, his shoulders hunched and his face grey.

Reaching the gate he said quietly, 'Yes Mr Grothe what do you want?'

'I'm sorry to disturb you,' William replied. 'I heard that your wife was very ill and came to say how sorry I was to hear that. I hope she recovers soon. I won't disturb you any longer, I'll go now.'

'My wife died a short while ago,' said Hartanto. His voice was curiously flat and unemotional, sounding empty.

'Oh God I'm so sorry to hear that, so very, very sorry,' William turned and walked away. What more could he say?

A few days later, on arriving at his house after work, William was surprised to find Putri waiting to see him. At first he didn't know whether to be pleased to see her there or not. He certainly felt a bit apprehensive because he had filed Putri in a drawer somewhere, locked it and thrown away the key. He had managed to shut down the feelings she had engendered in him and now here she was stirring up them up again.

Also, there was the issue of her mother's death which could add to the volatility of the whole situation. So tentatively he approached his veranda wondering what he was going to say. He felt sympathy for her yet at the same time he was still angry with her for her rudeness in not contacting him before she went away. He knew it was petty of him but he was a stubborn man who found it difficult to let things go.

Shyly Putri held out her hand. 'Hello William,' she said, 'I've missed you.'

With those words, all anger and irritation that he had felt about her evaporated away. He took her hand in his and the memory of the first touch in her garden of those soft, cool fingers came flooding back.

'I'm so sorry about your mother.'

Her eyes filled with tears. 'Thank you. It was dengue fever.'

William nodded. 'How is your father?'

'He's not very well. We can't get him to eat anything,' she replied. 'He just sits and looks at a painting of my mother and smokes cigarettes. Sometimes he cries, it's awful to see. He loved my mother very much. I don't think he can live without her.'

'Come in.' He opened the door. 'I'll make some tea.' He had a moment of déjà vu, this was just like the last time he had seen her.

After he had served the tea and they were sitting together, there was a silence. Outside he could hear some chicks piping away. William sensed that the silence was welcome to Putri. It was a moment of calm for her in the pain of her situation.

'Do you remember when you were here before and we talked about books?' he eventually asked.

For a moment her face lit up at the memory. Then she sighed. 'I'm sorry I never came to see you again but someone saw me leave your house and told my father. He was very angry and sent me to stay with my auntie. I couldn't contact you to let you know. You must have thought it very rude of me.'

William blushed. 'No, not at all,'

Putri smiled, probably guessing the truth.

He poured some more tea to cover his embarrassment. His hands shook slightly as he thought, my god, what's the matter with me?

'Will you be returning to your aunts?'

Putri thought for a moment. It seemed to William that in those few seconds his whole life hung in a balance.

'No, I don't think so,' she answered slowly. 'Father needs me right now.'

'Oh good!' he blurted out. 'I mean it's good that you're not going away.'

Putri smiled shyly.

'What I mean is that I will be able to see more of you.' William burbled on.

By now he was in a terrible state and had no control of what was coming out of his mouth. With enormous effort, he tried to think of something to say that didn't make him sound like a blithering idiot.

'Haven't you brothers and sisters that can help?'

'Yes, three brothers but they're married and have families of their own to look after.'

'But what about you?' Putri looked puzzled as though she couldn't understand what he had just said.

'It is my duty,' she said simply.

William fell silent. He understood her devotion to her father but his heart screamed 'YOU ARE SACRIFICING YOURSELF'. He kept quiet. Having found her again he didn't want to lose her through a stupid comment.

Like most unsaid thoughts, it nestled in his mind causing an uncomfortable barrier of silence between them. It didn't last long. She quickly finished her tea and rose to her feet.

'I must go.'

'Yes,' said William. Then impulsively he clutched her hands.

'Please come to see me soon.'

She bent her head and kissed his fingers.

'Thank you William. You are so kind to me.' Then she hurried out of the door.

William watched her until she was out of sight. He stood for a long time as the dusk deepened and watched the Papatong in their hundreds and thousands feeding on the mosquitoes and the swifts swooping in their choreographed ballet of flight. Across the sky dark shapes flitted as the bats emerged, glimpsed momentarily.

The strong call of the muezzin hung in the air like the pungent scent of opium. William was a Protestant by upbringing but not fanatical in his belief. Religion was what you did on Sundays, a habit. He was a bit out of the habit as there were no churches close to where he lived. He really could do without a long and tiring journey on the one day when he allowed himself some rest. Religion for him was comfortable and soothing. If taken occasionally, just like a drug. If taken repeatedly and addictively, religion controlled body and mind, demanding more and more – again just like a drug.

Religion did not fill a void for him. He did not need it to numb the fear of existence. But the thought of religion now, or more specifically the thought of the religion of Islam, worried him. Putri was Muslim and he had lived enough time in Indonesia to recognise that Islam was unbending in its demands. There was no compromise. What demands would it make of him? Was he mad to even contemplate a relationship with a Muslim woman? But even as he thought about this he knew it was a waste of time. Contemplation didn't even enter into it; he was lost, adrift and hopelessly in love with her.

For the next few weeks, Putri visited William quite regularly whenever she could get away from looking after her father, who was in an unchanged state since the death of his wife. His grief seemed unending and an appalling air of gloom and sadness hung over their household. William was delighted to provide a place of refuge for her to escape to. They talked about books and laughed together. She told him about her love of plants and he listened fascinated, hypnotised by her voice and movement. He discovered that she was the only daughter with three brothers who were all married.

Sometimes she'd say, 'Now it's your turn I think. I want to hear all about Holland.'

William explained that much of the land was below the sea and that they built walls called dykes to keep the sea back. He was very dismissive about Holland's flatness and praised the beauty of Indonesia's mountains. Putri shook her head,

'Yes but I would love to see your country too.'

'I know what you'd like.' he said. 'The tulip festival.' He described the colours and shapes of all the thousands of tulips, reds, yellows, oranges, whites, pinks. Putri sat in awe as he described it all. She wished so much to see it for herself.

William felt his heart race as he watched her animated heart-shaped face and her joy at all his descriptions and stories of Holland. His self-control was gradually slipping away. Then one day, they walked on to the veranda and just when she was leaving, he pulled her to him and kissed her passionately.

'I'm so sorry Putri, so sorry. I should never have done that. Please forgive me.' She had turned away, looking flustered and run quickly for the gate. Shocked at what he'd done, his face hot he'd rushed back indoors and poured himself a large whisky, then another.

The hammering on his door woke William. He fumbled for his watch on the bedside table and squinted in the grey early morning light. Six o'clock. He was normally up and running by now but he'd drunk a bit too much brandy the night before. He hauled himself out of bed and staggered to his front door cursing as he caught his ankle on a chair leg. Outside a drizzly, misty rain had covered everything with a grey uniformity, he saw through the window. The hammering continued, insistent and demanding.

'Wait damn you, I'm coming.'

William flung open the door angrily then stopped in shock. 'Good God, what are you doing here?'

'Hello William. What a welcome! You don't sound very pleased to see me. Aren't you going to invite me in? I'm absolutely soaking wet. I thought Indonesia was supposed to be a country of sunshine.' All this was rattled off with the speed and precision of a Gatling gun.

Without waiting for a reply, the tall young woman who bore a striking resemblance to him, with the same blue eyes, strode past him.

'Tell them to bring my luggage in will you William?'

It was a question but had more of the tone of an order about it. Only now William became aware that there were several very wet Indonesians standing there with what seemed to him to be a mountain of luggage. He also noticed that they all had the same expression; one of recently being run over by a very large steamroller.

In a hung-over blur, William organised the

bringing in of the luggage and the payment of the porters. When he finally shut the door, he turned to find that his sister, for that was who the young woman was, had disappeared into his kitchen and was busily filling a kettle and putting water onto boil. She had also discarded her wet jacket which he gingerly picked up and hung over the back of a chair.

Feeling very like he had just gone several rounds with the heavyweight champion of the world, William stepped into the lounge and flopped into a chair. He took a couple of deep breaths to try and get up to speed with the whole bizarre situation.

His sister, Sophia, came and stood in the kitchen doorway and smiled at him. 'Poor William,' she said 'It must be a bit of a shock for you me turning up like this.'

William could only nod in reply; speech had still deserted him.

'But it was all a spur of the moment decision really and then I thought wouldn't it be a nice surprise if I just turned up with no warning. It is a nice surprise isn't it William? You are pleased to see me?'

'Um, yes of course Sophia. I'm delighted.' He shook his head to clear the fog and passed his hands over his eyes. 'But why on earth didn't you give me some warning? I have no room prepared and hardly any food in the house.'

'Yes I noticed,' she said dryly. Then impulsively she crossed the room and hugged him.

'Oh William it's so nice to see you, I've missed you so much. We never knew what was happening to you, your letters were so infrequent.'

William grinned and hugged her back. 'I'm sorry,' he said, 'I'm not a good letter writer.'

The kettle started to whistle and William started to get out of his chair but his sister was already in the kitchen rattling cups and teapot. For an instant a slight spasm of irritation crossed his face, he did like his privacy and an order to his life. Interference was the last thing he enjoyed. Then he smiled as he heard her singing. It was wonderful to see Sophia, he did so love her.

Later that day, after they had fixed Sophia up in one of the spare bedrooms and found wardrobes for her clothes and hats, 'enough to set someone up in a milliners' thought William, he asked a question that had been niggling on and off all day.

'Sophia, don't take this the wrong way as it's wonderful to see you, but why are you here?'

She pointed to her easel by way of explanation as she had her mouth full of watermelon.

He was perplexed. 'To paint? You've come all the way to Indonesia to paint?'

Sophia nodded as she busily attacked another slice of watermelon.

'But what about your job, at the school?'

'I just told them I was leaving,' she said wiping her mouth. 'That was absolutely delicious. Anyway it's all your fault you know.'

'What do you mean my fault?'

'Now don't get yourself in a state brother dear, calm down,' she said. It was one of your letters that did it shortly after you arrived in Indonesia. You were describing all the colours and the sights and the mountains and it made me wish so much to see it all, to paint it. So one day I just decided to come. I handed in my notice, packed my brushes and here I am.'

William smiled at the carefree, almost flippant way this was said. He could imagine the shock and consternation this must have caused the honest burghers who ran the school. They came from a small town where people led ordinary lives and the most exciting event was the annual market and craft fair. His job in Indonesia was a local talking point for months before and after leaving Holland.

Their parents had brought both him and Sophia up to be independent. They didn't have much choice with Sophia as she had always shown a very headstrong nature from a young age. She was always completely in control of her life and knew exactly what she wanted and where she was going. This independence had stood her and William in good stead as their parents had passed away a few years previously after a particularly vicious epidemic of influenza had killed many people in Holland.

William watched Sophia striding to and fro from the kitchen in that self-assured way that she had, healthy, active and full of purpose. She had always been the volatile one out of the pair of them, impulsively doing things, while he would take time to think things through.

Luckily it was a Sunday, the one day that he allowed himself some free time, hence the brandy the night before. Unfortunately his head felt like a turnip and his brain was non-existent so the careful thought that this completely unexpected situation required, just wasn't happening.

'You okay for money?' he suddenly asked Sophia.

'You are a sweetie William,' she smiled. 'Yes, I've got loads, saved a lot from my job and still got all the money mum and dad left us.'

Next day, the sun rose high in a clear blue sky

and the lush tropical vegetation steamed as the soaking tropical rain of the day before started to dry out.   Putri was walking up the path to William's house when she heard a woman singing in Dutch. The woman suddenly stopped singing and called out in Dutch

'William, darling, come and look at this absolutely enormous beetle in your kitchen.'

Putri stopped and her heart froze. She understood enough Dutch to pick up what was said, especially 'darling'. William had spoken the word in Dutch once in reference to his parents and she had asked its meaning.

Since her last visit, she had thought of nothing else but how he had taken her in his arms. That kiss, so gentle but so firm. She was visiting him again eagerly wanting to tell him that she felt the same way towards him, now this! How could she be so stupid? He had never given any indication there was anyone else, let alone that he was married. Yet the woman had clearly called him 'darling'. Confused, she turned to go when William strode onto his patio with Sophia following. At first they didn't see Putri as they were too busy shooing a gigantic stag beetle off into the garden.

Then William noticed Putri hurrying away.

'Putri wait, where are you going?' he called out and rushed down the path after her. She didn't stop so he grabbed her arm but she pulled away.

'Leave me William,' she said with tears in her eyes.

William was stunned. 'Putri, whatever is the matter?' he asked.

'Why did you not tell me about your wife?' she demanded.

He looked completely dumbfounded. 'My wife? What wife?'

'She' Putri pointed at Sophia accusingly.

William threw back his head and roared with laughter.

'Now you laugh at me,' said Putri. 'Goodbye William.'

'Before you go Putri, maybe you would like to meet my sister, Sophia,' he was still chuckling. 'Remember I told you about her.'

Putri's jaw dropped, 'Your sister, the teacher.'

'The very same one. Though now it seems it's my sister the travelling artist.'

'What terrible fibs are you telling about me William?' Sophia had strolled up to them and had only caught the tail end of what William had said.

Holding out her hand, she smiled at Putri and said 'I'm Sophia, William's sister.'

Putri took the hand and shook it, her

mouth still gaping in surprise.

'William,' Sophia turned to her brother, 'are you going to introduce us sometime in the near future or are we going to stand here forever.'

'Oh Lord, excuse me,' he said. 'Sophia this is Putri and Putri this is my impossible sister Sophia.'

'Well come inside Putri and tell me all about yourself,' Sophia took Putri gently by the arm and lead her towards the house. As they walked, Sophia glanced over at William and smiled archly at him, causing him to blush crimson to the roots of his hair.

Inside the house, Putri and William avoided eye contact, but there was no hiding the electric current between them. Sophie's smile grew broader as she looked between them. William, flustered, rushed into the kitchen to put the kettle on. still blushing furiously and behaving in a meticulously polite way.

'Well, what have I stumbled into?' She was laughing as she took her cup of tea from William's shaking fingers. William winced and shook his head. He had no idea how to deal with his sister's innuendos. Luckily Putri didn't seem to notice and in fact she and Sophia were getting on famously, chatting away together like old friends. William left them to it and went to the kitchen to get some fruit. Sophie came in soon after to help him.

'Well William,' she went to the drawer to get a sharp knife to cut up the fruit. 'You dark horse. No wonder you didn't write, you've obviously had other things on your mind.'

'I don't know what you mean,' William spoke in his best off hand manner.

Sophia laughed, smiling sweetly at him. 'She's very beautiful,' then went back to join Putri.

After their tea, Sophia excused herself saying there was a flower she had seen that she wanted to sketch. She picked up her pad and smiled warmly at Putri.

'Bye for now. I'll see you very soon, I expect.' She laughed and strode out the door into the sunshine.

William looked nervously over at Putri. They spoke at the same time and then both laughed. The awkwardness between them relaxed. William spoke first.

'I'm so sorry about the last time I saw you. I should not have …. grabbed you like that. I hope you can forgive me.'

'Oh William there is nothing to forgive. I feel the same way about you.' Putri moved forward and took his hand, smiling shyly.

'You do!' exclaimed William. 'Oh Putri my darling'

Then they were in each other's arms.

Sophia who was listening outside the door smiled to herself and then quietly went off to sketch her fictitious plant.

William snapped awake, aware immediately that something was very wrong. He could hear shouts and screams from outside. One word in particular stuck out, 'Gempa! Gempa! Gempa!'

Then he felt it. The room lurched and he was almost flung off his bed.

'William what's happening?' He heard Sophia calling,

'Earthquake! Earthquake' he shouted. ' Get outside quick!'

He had felt minor tremors before but this one was big. The house shook again, growling like an angry bear. the force of the earthquake flung him across the bedroom and he bounced off a wall. He managed to stay on his feet and grabbed the trousers and shirt that he had taken off the night before. Somehow he managed to put them on and holding onto a chest of drawers to stop himself from falling over, he jammed his feet into a pair of shoes. Heading for his front door, he collided with Sophia who had a look of pure terror on her face.

He knew how she felt; there was something elemental about the whole experience. They had no control whatsoever over what was happening. It was as if some enormous giant was flicking them with his fingers and at any moment would bring his fist crashing down. Then he noticed that she was struggling to carry several canvasses plus her paints and goodness knows what else.

'What in God's name are you doing Sophia? Leave that stuff, save yourself.'

She ignored him, if anything gripped them even tighter and headed for the door with a determined look on her face. William knew that look, it was irreversible. At that moment the ground shifted again and the floor of the house tilted, luckily towards the front door so they were more or less shunted out onto the patio. Without pausing they let their momentum carry them down the path away from the house. Finally they stopped and turned.

What they saw was horrific. The house was swaying back and forth as if the walls were fluid but it was the sound more than anything. The walls were groaning in agony as if alive. Then they shuddered in a climax and the whole structure disintegrated and caved in.

From further down the path nearer the Kampong, screams and people moaning and sobbing could be heard. Children were crying and the sky was lit up from numerous fires.

'We must go and help them William.'

Sophia dumped her things under a tree and turned towards the path.

Her brother strode after her, as she broke into a trot, panting to keep up. 'Yes, nothing we can do about our stuff for now.'

They headed towards the Kampong. The first few houses they came to were completely demolished, a mixture of wood, bamboo and stone tossed and strewn around. A woman, absolutely distraught, was clawing at the debris. William and Sophia soon realised that her child or children were buried under it and soon were heaving chunks of rubble away. Miraculously they heard a child calling out and found a little girl safe under a strong hardwood table that had taken the weight of falling tiles and masonry. They brushed off the woman's thanks and moved on to where they could help next. The next few hours revealed a nightmare of devastation, as they moved through the Kampong helping where they could. It seemed that barely a house had been left complete.

The first crushed, mangled body of a child clutching a little rag doll which they pulled out of some wreckage, had Sophia sobbing uncontrollably. William went deathly pale but managed not to vomit. However as the night progressed and the body count grew they became curiously immune to the carnage around them. It was as though an emotional switch had clicked off to save them from the horror. For a moment, William stood back, watching Sophia handing over a tiny little girl, battered but still alive, to its mother. Tears were running streaks down Sophia's dusty face and he knew this whole experience would haunt both of them for ever.

At some point in the early morning hours, the merest hint of light brushing the horizon, William and Sophia sagged wearily on a small wall. They were past speech; they just held each other's hands for comfort. An old woman came out of a nearby house, one of the few that were reasonably intact, carrying a tray with two mugs of coffee, made the Indonesian way.

'Tuan, Ibu, kopi,' she bowed and offered the thick, black, sweet drink. Never did anything smell more inviting. William and Sophia fell upon the coffee.

William bowed back to the old woman,

'Hatur Nuhun ibu' he thanked her in Sundanese.

'Sami sami Tuan,' she replied and quietly went back inside her house.

Dawn came slowly and in the sweet light birds sang. As the birds sang and the sun warmed the air, William and Sophia looked at the devastation that the earthquake had caused.

Jumping suddenly to his feet, William

exclaimed, 'Putri! Oh my God, Putri!' He started off striding fast in the direction of her house.

'William wait,' called Sophia. 'I'll go with you.'

Sophia was running behind but William was walking like a man possessed. All his weariness had vanished.

When they reached Putri's house the full power of the earthquake was devastatingly displayed in the early morning light. Hartanto's magnificent mansion was a ruin. The beautiful garden was strewn with rubble. Trees and mature shrubs were uprooted and scattered around. The wall that surrounded the property was smashed, broken and the Morning Glory that William admired so much was destroyed. Then they saw Putri sitting on the ground. She was holding her father's head in her lap and crying soundlessly. They approached tentatively afraid of intruding on her private grief. They stood silently until she looked up.

'Oh William,' she sobbed.

In those two words was all the pain and suffering that a person could feel. In an instant William was on his knees with his arms around her, helping her lay her father's body gently onto the ground. She cried quietly into his shoulder as Sophia stood and looked on, sharing Putri's pain.

After a while Putri began to speak.

'When the earthquake came everyone ran out into the garden. Father was very confused but the servants helped me and we got him away from the house. It was horrible William our lovely house just broke before our eyes. Then father started calling mother's name and struggled to get away. We couldn't hold him and he broke free and ran back into the house. I followed him. I was scared William. Everything was falling and then I saw him with my mother's painting. He had gone to get the painting of my mother. I ran to him and helped him with it. It was so heavy because of the frame but we carried it. We were almost out of the house when something falling hit father on the head. I don't know how but I dragged father and the painting outside and away from the house. Then I passed out. When I came to, I saw our servants had bathed father's head but his face was very white and he lay quiet on the ground. I went to him and held him. He smiled at me and said,

"Imik". He called me by my mother's name.' She sighed.

"Imik," he said. 'You are so beautiful.'

Then he touched my face and smiled. 'Kiss me Imik,' he said.

'I kissed him, William. I kissed my father and he died.'

Putri bent down and gently stroked her father's face with tears streaming from her eyes. William picked her up and held her tightly to him as Sophie sobbed beside them.

After the earthquake William saw a side of the Indonesian people that he had not seen before. They grieved deeply and passionately, then quickly buried their dead. They quietly rebuilt their houses and their lives. They did it all with gentle humour and even a few smiles. Their quiet resilience against the awesome might that nature had thrown against them was noble. William found himself re-evaluating judgements and opinions that he had begun to make about Indonesia and its people. He still found them full of contrasts and surprises. One minute they really could astound him with their silly foolishness. Then with the next breath they could show a phlegmatic tolerance and charm and a gentle acceptance of life that was inspiring and humbling.

After the earthquake, William contacted the army and organised a mass distribution of tents and blankets to those in need, including him and Sophia.

Putri buried her father. Her brothers and their families came. All the local people turned up even though many of them had just buried members of their own families. What slightly surprised William was the number of people who made the journey from surrounding districts to show their respect. Hartanto was obviously very well known, even greatly admired.

At the funeral, Putri introduced William to her family as a business associate of her father. She never once gave the slightest hint that there was anything between them. William did detect a coolness of attitude from Putri's brothers but it did not bother him. He quietly gave his commiserations and then kept a very low profile. He also noticed a deference from Putri to her brothers and what seemed to him to be a superior attitude from them to her. He put this down to the formality of the situation.

When he said his goodbyes, he managed to pull Putri to one side.

'How are you?' he whispered out of the side of his mouth, feeling a bit like a gangster in a cheap novel.

Putri involuntarily giggled and had to quickly cover her mouth with her hand. 'I'm ok William but my brothers want me to go back with them tonight.'

'What!' exclaimed William, 'You're not going are you?'

'No,' said Putri. 'My brothers are very

angry about this but they cannot force me to go with them. This is my home. I have to stay while the house is being repaired.' Putri had insisted on having one of the army tents and putting it up in her garden, with her old nanny.

'Ok,' William whispered, 'I will visit you after your brothers have gone.' He was still speaking out of the corner of his mouth and it pleased him to see the humour had returned to her eyes. Then he left.

Later that night, he strolled through the Kampong towards Putri's house. He noticed many people stopping to greet him with a warmth he had never felt before. People came out of their houses to wave and acknowledge him. Obviously the help he and Sophia had given had not gone unnoticed. Sophia had started teaching a few curious children who had come to watch her paint and this had soon developed into what seemed to William to be all the children in the Kampong. Every morning there were shrieks of laughter and songs coming from Sophia's class. He had also made the decision to cut the time spent working on the water way to give people a chance to heal their shattered lives and rebuild their houses.

When he reached Putri's garden, William saw her cooking food over a wood fire. The nanny was chopping vegetables and Putri was frying something in a wok. They were laughing together over some joke. He called out first not to startle them and Putri looked up, smiled and beckoned him over. He went over and sat next to the fire and warmed his hands.

'Selamat malam nenek,' he said to the old woman. She smiled back at him and nodded.

'What are you cooking?' he asked Putri.

'Fried tempeh and vegetables in soy sauce,' she said. 'Would you like some?'

'I've already eaten, thank you,' William replied. 'It smells delicious.' Then with a slight note of surprise in his voice, 'I didn't know you could cook.'

She smiled at him teasingly, 'Yes, I can cook' she said. 'I can also sew and wash clothes.'

William blushed.

'When I was younger,' said Putri, 'my mother sent me to stay with my grandmother. She taught me many things.'

'Oh right,' was all William could think of to say. Then he remembered why he had come. 'What happened with your brothers?,' he asked. 'Were there any problems?'

Putri did not say anything for a while, she just stirred the food. Then she looked directly at William, the smile had left her face. 'They want to find me a husband,' she said.

William looked startled. 'Find you a husband? I don't understand…. when?'

The old woman put the chopped vegetables in the wok and Putri started stirring again, this time a lot more angrily. 'My brothers say that it is time I was married and that it is not right for me to stay here alone. I bring shame on the family. So they will choose a husband for me.'

'Surely they can't force you to marry someone you don't want to?'

Putri laughed bitterly. 'They are my older brothers and I must do what they decide.'

'I might be able to understand that if you were a young girl,' said William, 'but you're a woman, perfectly capable of making decisions for yourself. Good God Putri it's medieval!'

'You don't understand William; they will bring great pressure on me. Family pressure, social pressure and religious pressure, all these they will use to make me do what they decide.'

'And your wishes? They don't ask what you want?'

'No,' said Putri. 'I must do what they say or go and live in domestic servitude with them where I will have no life. Oh yes, I forget, there is one more choice. If I do not do what they say, I can live here as an outcast where people will think bad of me and treat me like a crazy woman.'

'Who the hell cares what people think?'

William's voice was angry and it made the old nanny and Putri jump. 'And you do have a choice, a very good choice, you can marry me.'

There, I've said it, thought William. It's out. This is when Putri quietly turns me down and I walk away with my tail between my legs.

Putri looked at William with astonishment. Then she smiled gently at him. 'Oh William my darling, I am Muslim.'

She left the statement trailing in the air. They both knew what she meant. The unsaid implications and difficulties were obvious.

'So what!' exclaimed William recklessly. 'To hell with it all, let's just get married.'

'But William,' said Putri, 'Muslim must marry Muslim and you are Christian, I cannot marry you. You would have to become Muslim.'

'To hell with that,' snorted William. 'We can have a civil ceremony. That will make it legal.'

'Not in the eyes of my people, William,' Putri pleaded. 'We would be living in sin.'

William didn't reply. He stared for a long time into the flames of the fire. Putri's eyes begged him to understand.

The old woman sat quietly listening to all that was said. She couldn't understood their words but she was watching them both intently. Quietly she rescued the forgotten food and placed it aside. Unobtrusively she sat back and patiently waited, her old, lined face full of concern for the young woman she had looked after as a child and watched grow up over the years.

Finally William let out a deep sigh and stood up. 'I love you Putri,' he said simply. 'I want you to be my wife. If you cannot be my wife in Indonesia, so be it. We can live in Holland or anywhere else you like but we will be together.' Then he asked, 'I must know Putri, do you love me? I must know this, do you?'

By now tears were rolling down Putri's face but she smiled at William as she said, 'Oh yes, yes I do.'

'Then if I love you and you love me that is all that really matters, isn't it?' said William. 'Think about what I have said, we can make it work Putri.'

Then he turned and walked quietly back through the kampong, deep in thought, barely acknowledging the people along the way.

For the next few days William didn't see Putri. He couldn't decide whether that was a good or bad sign. He had told Sophia what Putri had said about her brothers and that he had said they'd better not dare tell her who she could or could not marry!

'Oh for goodness sake William calm down,'

Sophia exclaimed one day after her brother had stood up, sat down and paced around for the umpteenth time in as many minutes.

'I'm sorry.' William shook his head. 'It's been three days now Sophia and not a sign. I think she's turned me down. Her brothers have forced her to marry someone, I know it. It's been too much for her.'

Sophia burst out laughing. 'Oh William, think of what you're asking her to do. It's a huge step for her. To leave her country and her home, her family, everything that she knows. She must have time to think it through. It took you three months before finally deciding to come to Indonesia, remember?'

'Yes I know,' replied William, 'but, but, oh to hell with it I'm going to see her. I must know what her decision is.'

When William reached Putri's garden, she wasn't there. Her old nanny was sweeping the area outside the tent. In halting Indonesian William asked her where Putri was and was shocked to find that she had gone to visit her brothers. Further questioning revealed that the nanny didn't know when Putri would be returning. William was now more confused than ever.

Over the next few days he concentrated on his work and focused on the canal which was nearing completion. Then one evening when he came home after work, he found Sophia and Putri talking and laughing together. As soon as Putri saw him, she jumped up and ran to him. William dropped his bag and hugged her tightly to him. He kissed her unrestrainedly.

'Well?' he asked.

'Oh yes, yes, yes, William. We will go to Holland and I will be your wife,' she said.

William burst out laughing and did a little jig making Putri laugh.

'I take it you two are getting married,' called out Sophia.

'Yes we are,' said William grabbing hold of Putri and swinging her around so her feet left the ground making her shriek out in delight.

Later while the three of them were sitting, Putri told of her visit to her brothers. She had gone to discuss with them the idea of her marriage to William. She knew they wouldn't sanction it, but she hoped to get some sort of blessing from them as she would be leaving Indonesia and wouldn't see them for a long while. They were furious and demanded that she immediately break off relations with William, stay with them and receive religious instruction to atone for her sin while they found her a husband. All the while hinting darkly that a good husband would be difficult to get as she was now 'soiled goods'.

Putri had expected opposition, she had expected them to be difficult and angry but she hadn't expected quite the radical vehemence she received. It was their reaction and the obvious low esteem with which they regarded her that convinced Putri there was no further life for her with the remnants of her family. The attitude of the rest of her family, aunts, uncles and cousins would be poisoned by her brothers and Putri could see that soon her life in Indonesia would be one of unhappy drudgery. She had already decided that she wanted to be with William, so her family's negative views made the next step of leaving Indonesia and going to live in Holland that much easier. She didn't trust her brothers not to use force to keep her there. So without giving any warning she had quietly slipped away and come straight to William and Sophia. When she explained her worry about being followed, William jumped up, striding back and forth across the room.

'Right you're moving here!'

Putri started to protest but William was adamant.

'No, I'll get your tent brought up here in the morning. I insist on it.'

Putri shut up at that, 'Yes William,' she said demurely. 'Thank you.'

'They'll have Sophia and me to deal with if they try any funny business,' said William in a grim, determined way.

So worried was he that he insisted Putri sleep that night in Sophia's tent. Very early next morning William was up and away to the canal. He soon returned with half a dozen strong workers. Putri insisted on going with William to her garden as she was concerned for her nanny. William left one of his workers with Sophia to help clear and prepare a space for Putri's tent and belongings.

They returned without incident and Putri's nanny far from being upset with the move seemed to positively relish it. She had a sparkle in her eyes and a spring in her step. Her sharp tongue and bustling body kept the workers to task and soon their tent was erected with what few possessions they had, tidied away.

Amongst those were the painting of Putri's mother and a large studio photograph of her parents which she had found relatively unscathed amongst the ruins. The nanny had also rescued a large doll with golden hair and a lacy bonnet - a toy from Putri's childhood. While Putri was visiting her brothers the nanny had found it, in a still intact bedroom at the back of the broken house.

As soon as Sophia saw it, she fell in love with it and made many sketches of it. When William teased her about it, she said,

'I'm going to paint a large still life with this

doll in it. You shall have it for a wedding gift.'

That night around the campfire was a happy interlude in what had been a traumatic and painful couple of months. They laughed and planned for the future and somehow their laughter and their love for each other dissolved any unhappiness around them. The canal was all but finished and William was keen to 'tie the knot', as he put it, with Putri.

He offered to take the nanny back to Holland with them but she wished to go and stay with her sister who lived by the sea in a little fishing village called Pangandaran. William promised to leave her enough money to buy a small plot of land and live comfortably for many years to come. Sophia sketched the nanny by the light of the fire and later gave her the sketch. The nanny was quite overcome and kept stealing looks at it and exclaiming delightedly.

'Why Jansen Grothe?' asked William, looking at the signature. 'Why not Sophia Grothe?'

'I've decided to use just our family name,' Sophia replied. 'That way people won't know whether it's painted by a man or woman.'

'Will you come with us to Holland?' Putri asked Sophia.

'No, I'm going to Bali,' said Sophia.

'Bali!' William sounded surprised. 'Why

Bali?'

'I hear there are many artists in Bali and it is supposed to be very beautiful,' Sophia smiled. 'Then after Bali, who knows?' Sophia flung her arms in the air dramatically. They all laughed, including the nanny who hadn't understood any of what was said. She was just laughing because she was happy about her picture.

The next afternoon, Putri's brothers came striding angrily up the path to the tents shouting at Putri. The eldest brother came forward aggressively as if to get hold of Putri but hesitated when he saw both William and Sophia stepping forward to bar his way. Like most bullies, when he was challenged, the fizz went out of the pop. The other brothers started shouting again egging him on so he pushed forward attempting to shove Sophia out of the way. That was his mistake; Sophia's right arm shot back and then forward, her balled fist connecting with his nose. He crumpled back shocked and hurt. In the stunned silence that followed this, Putri's nanny stepped forward and to everyone's astonishment told the brothers to leave. She spoke quietly but firmly and with great dignity. She reviled them for their actions and behaviour to Putri and said they were the ones who had brought shame on themselves and the Indonesian people, not Putri. Then she turned, took Putri by the arm and led her into their tent.

Now completely demoralised the brothers went off muttering and throwing imprecations over their shoulders as they went.

William turned to Sophia. 'Nice punch,' he said with a smile.

She grinned back. 'It's what you learn growing up with an older brother.'

'Putri come out now, they've gone,' called William.

Putri came out with her nanny and ran over and hugged William and Sophia.

'Sorry about hitting your brother,' said Sophia, 'but he shouldn't have pushed me.'

Putri giggled covering her mouth with her hand. She looked at Sophia with awe.

Both William and Sophia hugged and kissed the nanny. She got quite flustered, brushed them off and busied herself making the fire for cooking.

Putri, William and Sophia stood and watched the evening drawing in.

'Look at all the dragon flies,' said Sophia.

'The Sundanese people call them Papatong,' said William.

Some children appeared in the garden, running about and playing. Soon one of the boys was making the Papatong dance before them.

'How do they do that?' asked Sophia.

'Magic!' said William and Putri together then they both laughed.

[This painting is signed 'Jansen Grothe'. It was actually painted by Sophie Jacoba Wilhelmina Jansen-Grothe, a nineteenth century Dutch artist. It was bought long ago by David and his first wife, in Cape Town, South Africa. They found it at the back of a second-hand furniture shop and paid R6 for it.]

If you have enjoyed reading this book, it would help sales enormously if you would give it a review – a star rating and a line would be great.

Go to the book's page on Amazon. Find **Papatong** by David Powell Davies and scroll down until you find 'Reviews'.

Then find 'Write a review'. The more reviews the better the ranking on Amazon.

Thank you so much.

About the author

David Powell Davies

18-03-1949 – 30-07-2018

David wrote short stories for many years. Recently he completed his first novel. He wrote two film scripts, the first was shortlisted by the British Film Institute. The second was a work in progress. He wrote, in collaboration with an American songwriter (Lorna Lee) a musical called 'The Kissing Screen.' It was performed once on stage in the 90s. He also wrote several stage plays and pilots for TV.

David was born in Hong Kong and grew up in Wales and Africa (Nigeria and Uganda). He graduated from the Royal Academy of Dramatic Art (RADA) in 1972 and then worked as an actor for 28 years – for two of those years in South Africa (1975-8).

In 2000, David moved overseas after obtaining his CELTA qualification to teach English language. He taught English in Singapore, China and in Indonesia and is fondly remembered by his many students in those countries. After a while, he settled in Indonesia, remarried and had a son.

In July 2018, after a short illness, David passed away. He is survived by his wife Reni and 13 year old son, his two adult daughters from his previous marriage, his grandson and his brother.

David lives on in the hearts and minds of all his family and friends, who loved him dearly. He will be missed.

Proceeds from the sale of this book will go to David's son's education.

Here's a taster from Dave's Novel which will be published towards the end of next year 2019 ....

He wrote:

This is the first chapter of a novel about time.

It is also about families at different times of their existence. In their pasts, in their futures, in their now and in their parallel lives. These families are from different continents, different cultures but through marraige and travel they connect with each other.

The novel opens at this time, the beginning of the 21st century where we meet an Indonesian connection. Soon the time shifts to early 20th century. We see the beginning of this family and their connection with the energy source that will change their lives.

Time is impermanent. It is not linear, it shifts and changes with the creation of thought.

We live our lives in a linear framework of time because we find it convenient for our existence.

But what if...?

THE HEART OF STONE

Chapter One

Mama had a Go'ib stone that was in the shape of a serpent. It was given to her or rather it chose her. This stone has a spirit entity living in it, a Go'ib. The stone was passed on to her by her father, my grandfather. He was a very powerful, highly respected man and was held in awe by the people of his kampung.

Every Monday and Thursday night she would conduct a ritual with the stone out of respect for the entity within it. The stone brought protection to the house. If she forgot to conduct the ritual, for whatever reason (maybe she was tired or too busy) the stone made its presence felt. It did this in many ways, objects would move around the house, you would put something down and when you went to get it later it would be somewhere else. Alsoat night people would hear noises, footsteps, doors opening and shutting but there would be no one there and these things would continue until we got fed up and would scream at mama,

'Mama please look to the stone, it's driving us crazy.'

Eventually Mama got too old and absent minded to give the stone the amount of attention it required. She told her older brother about this. He was a psychic and was regularly called upon to cleanse houses that had unwanted and troublesome spirits in them. He suggested that it was probably time for the stone to move on. The only problem with this was that the stone couldn't just be given away; it chose where it wanted to go.

'Don't be ridiculous,' said Fahad my boyfriend, 'A stone can't choose it's not a sentient being.'

I shut my diary quickly and turned on him. 'Didn't anyone tell you it's rude to read over someone's shoulder? Anyway what does sentient mean?'

Fahad laughed. It was his put down laugh with a toss of his head and a roll of his eyes. I hated it. 'It means seeing and feeling,' he said. 'And a stone can't do either.'

'How do you know Mr Clever know it all' I said. 'The laws of physics say that a bee cannot fly, that its body is too big for its wings, but it flies, doesn't it?'

Fahad's face hardened, 'You talk such crap,' he said and walked out.

I waited until I was sure he had gone and then I went to my wardrobe and felt around under my folded underwear. I found the stone and took it out. You see, it had chosen me.

I looked at the coiled serpent sitting in the palm of my hand and the carved scales on its skin seemed to move. It felt hot on my skin. My younger brother had wanted it and so had my sister but mama had told them firmly that it was not for them. She knew that they would use the stone for personal gain and the power it would give them. One day mama was burning incense and saying her blessings when she went into a trance. I was very worried as we were alone in the house but it did not last for long and she soon recovered. She finished the ritual and I brought her some tea. 'Sayang,' she said, 'It is yours now.' She picked up the stone and handed it to me.

I felt very afraid. 'Mama I do not want it,' I said, putting the stone down but try as I might I could not let it go.

'There,' said Mama with finality, 'It's chosen you.'

So from that moment I said the rituals and cared for the stone. I didn't tell anyone and neither did mama.

'It's gone,' was all she said if anyone asked.

You can stay in touch about pre-publication orders by joining the mailing lists at www.tambourinepress.com
Write to tambourinepress@yahoo.com and give your name and email address and we'll be in contact.